ALL OF THE PEOPLE Callie faced looked shocked.

As shocked as she was feeling.

If this was a dream, it was the strangest and most real dream she had ever had.

Some of the people around her started crying, some dropped to the floor and huddled with their heads down.

Everyone looked like they had been through a very, very hard day.

Some were dressed, some were naked and others were moving to cover the naked ones in blankets.

And the distinct smell of human death seemed to suddenly be everywhere.

Callie spun around, only to be faced with the most incredible sight she had ever seen.

An entire wall that looked like a window and seemed like a lot of movies she had seen shot from orbit.

Below her the Earth was slowly spinning past.

Not possible.

That view was too much for her to take.

She could feel the room growing faint and she started to slump to the ground, but strong hands caught her.

She mumbled "Thanks" before everything went black.

Also by

Dean Wesley Smith

The Seeders Universe:

Against Time

Sector Justice

Morning Song

The High Edge

The Thunder Mountain Universe:

Thunder Mountain

Monumental Summit

Avalanche Creek

The Edwards Mansion

Lake Roosevelt

Warm Springs

Melody Ridge

The Earth Protection League:

Life of a Dream

AGAINST TIME

A SEEDERS UNIVERSE NOVEL

DEAN WESLEY SMITH

*wmg*PUBLISHING

Against Time

Published 2015 by WMG Publishing
www.wmgpublishing.com
Published in a different form in *Smith's Monthly #3*,
December, 2013
Cover and Layout copyright © 2015 by WMG Publishing
Cover design by Allyson Longueira/WMG Publishing
Cover art copyright © 3000ad/Dreamstime
ISBN-13: 978-0-615-93523-2
ISBN-10: 0-615-93523-0

AGAINST TIME

A SEEDERS UNIVERSE NOVEL

PART ONE

1

CALLIE SHERIDAN felt a sense of relief that she could finally see the light ahead. More than she imagined she would feel, considering she had enjoyed the three days down in the Oregon Caves. A real change and a relief from her normal grind of research and teaching undergrad classes in Paleontology at the University of Oregon in Eugene.

But after three days completely in the dark and damp of the cave, she was ready to see some natural light once again, even if it was just a rainy Oregon day.

She and the two graduate students with her had gotten permission from the Forest Service to go into a special area of the Oregon Caves complex, far off the normal tourist trails. It had taken them almost four of hours of hiking just to get to the tiny room. There they had been allowed to dig for signs of fish skeletons preserved in the rocks of the cave.

One of the students, Jim Williams, was in his final year, working on his thesis, married, with a child in Eugene. He stood no more than five six, shorter than Callie by a couple of inches, and had bright red hair. From the pictures Callie had seen of his new child, the red hair had moved on a generation.

Barb Hillcrest still had over a year in school to get to her thesis. Barb was a solid woman and towered over Callie at over six feet. Barb lived alone with three cats and was worried about getting back to them.

Callie liked them both, and both had turned out to be hard, hard workers during the entire time in the cave. Both had focused their studies in vertebrate paleontology, which was Callie's specialty.

The Oregon Caves had been formed out of granite instead of normal limestone and was a gold mine for fossils from various times in history. It had taken her almost a year to get the permission from the Forest Service for the short surface dig. A cave specialist and park ranger named Dave had gone with them to make sure that they wouldn't disturb anything in the cave with their dig except around one small area tucked in the back of a small cave.

Dave was a middle-aged guy with a gut and gray hair and had a fantastic sense of humor that kept them laughing, even though he must have been bored to tears with their conversations at times and the excitements over finds of tiny fossils.

On the way in he had kept them entertained with his stories of the cave and the names of the different rooms and how they had been named. For a pretty long distance into the cave the path had been covered with asphalt and was an easy walk, with some stair climbing and one bridge over a stream called The River Styx.

Now they were all carrying out some great samples in their backpacks that would keep them busy for months at school. The trip was a great success and she honestly had no idea what they might have found.

Dave had decided that instead of having them climb out the tourist exit where the tours left, he'd have them just backtrack to the way they had come in. As they neared the front entrance to the cave, Dave suddenly shouted "Karen!" and ran forward.

He had been leading the group up the incline on the asphalt trail that wound through some rock fall, so Callie couldn't see what he had seen.

The light from the small cave opening was bright, even though it had an airlock on it. So someone must have left the door open.

Callie shielded her eyes, carefully watching her step as she went forward to make sure she stayed on the asphalt.

Suddenly both Barb and Jim ran up behind Dave, who was now kneeling over a woman who looked to be Dave's age. She also wore a park ranger uniform like Dave's. Her gray hair had been cut short and she looked like she had been beautiful in her day.

But now she was sprawled on the ground in the middle of the asphalt trail and to Callie she looked very dead.

And smelled dead as well.

Behind Karen, scattered along the trail were a dozen more people, all sprawled in various positions and all very dead. Clearly this Karen had been leading a walking tour into the cave with a bunch of tourists when something really awful happened.

Callie quickly checked out a couple of other bodies, an older couple wearing heavy coats. There were no obvious marks on them and no blood.

Callie stepped back and just stood, staring at the bodies, trying to make sense of what she was seeing.

He stomach was twisted into a knot and she wanted to just get sick. Never had she seen so much death in one place. Seeing something like this on television was something, standing here staring at the dead bodies and smelling the rot starting to take over was another matter completely.

Was this some sort of elaborate practical joke?

She looked around the rocks scattered through the cave mouth, but saw nothing that looked out of place.

Could someone have been this sick to do this sort of joke?

She moved back a few more steps closer to her two students and Dave where he now held Karen in his lap and was sobbing.

Callie had been around dead animals and a couple dead humans in her time, and this smell was very, very real and going to get worse, much worse, very soon. These people had been laying here dead for at least a day, maybe slightly longer.

How was that even possible, in the middle of a tourist attraction during a busy season?

As Callie looked along the group of dead, eleven men, women and one teenage boy, she could tell a few animals had worked at ones closest to the cave entrance, since it was braced open by the body of a man laying face down on the asphalt.

More than anything she wanted to be sick. This was not a pretty sight. But she had to stay clear in her thoughts for the moment. There would be time for reacting later.

She just couldn't imagine what might have caused this and why no one had come for these people and bodies.

This made no sense at all.

None.

She covered her nose with her sleeve and tried to think.

Then suddenly one very ugly word popped into her head.

Gas.

"We need to get out of here now!" she shouted to her students and Dave. "Move past the bodies quickly, don't look at them. Get up the trail to the parking lot."

"What do you think caused this?" Barb asked, clearly stunned, but moving.

"Might be gas," Callie said. "Jim, help me with Dave."

They both went to pull Dave away from the body of a woman named Karen, but he brushed them aside, angry.

"No, I'm staying with her."

"Dave," Callie said, "there's nothing you can do for her."

"I don't care," he said, looking up at Callie, his eyes full of tears. "She's my wife. I'm staying."

"We'll send help," Jim said.

Callie nodded, but doubted that they would find help as quickly as Jim made it sound. Something here was very, very wrong.

Callie motioned for Jim to follow Barb up the trail and past the bodies.

Without a look back at the man holding his very dead wife or at the bodies she passed, Callie followed her two graduate students up and into the light.

Outside the big trees looked normal, the day was beautiful, a slight breeze blowing among the pine.

It felt normal.

And that scared Callie even more.

All three of them took off running up the paved path through the trees, following the signs that said "Parking Lot."

It took them only a minute at full run for the three of them to reach the wide, paved parking lot.

Callie expected police and everything else to be there, but instead the lot felt deserted.

Two bodies lay sprawled near one car.

Around them the towering mountains stretched upwards, leaving most of the parking lot tucked into the side of the hill in shadow.

Callie made herself stop, take a deep breath to clear her mind, and then look around for anything that seemed wrong or out of place.

Nothing.

A beautiful afternoon in the Oregon Mountains.

Except for the two bodies sprawled in the parking lot.

"What happened?" Barb asked, her voice shaking.

It was clear Barb was barely holding it together. But Callie had no answers for her. All Callie could do was stand there on the edge of the parking lot, staring at the bodies and shaking her head.

She had no idea what had happened.

But she had no doubt now that this was a lot bigger than some poison gas in the mouth of a cave.

A lot bigger.

2

VARDIS FISHER sat in his big black inertia chair, holding on for dear life as his ship, *The Lady*, came from deep space way too hot and directly into orbit insertion around a big, green-and-blue planet they had named N-21-7.

He had no doubt his fingers were going to have to be pried from the soft foam of the armrests and it tasted like his stomach might revolt from the sharp garlic on artichoke pizza he had baked them for lunch.

Doc, sitting to his right in his inertia chair, had them braking like crazy to hold the orbit as the features of the planet flashed by far, far too fast for Fisher to even catch a glimpse. You would have thought they had someone with damn big guns on their ass.

Doc was skinny and over six foot, with a wide grin and blue eyes that seemed to almost twinkle at times. Fisher, on the other hand, stood about four inches shorter than Doc with a body one person in a gym called a perfect V-shape. Wide shoulders, narrow waist and he kept his brown hair cut very short and no beard or moustache, while Doc wore a wide moustache that seemed to just be expanding on his skinny face.

Doc's fingers were flying over his control panel. Fisher's job was to watch for anything in front of them in orbit, but as fast as Doc had them braking, their orbital trajectory just kept changing, so Fisher had no clue what was coming up, let alone be able to watch for anything.

They might hit something before they even had time to blink, and if the object they plowed into was too large, their screens might not block it.

This stunt was all his skinny partner's idea. Doc wanted to test out a new theory. He wanted to see how close to a planet they could drop out of a trans-tunnel and still control slowing into an orbit.

He had convinced Fisher to give it a try by saying, "Just never know when it might come in handy in the future."

Fisher was big on being prepared for just damn near anything, and they had been chased more than once in the last few years of roaming around through space. And more than likely it would happen again.

Besides, he figured that if they didn't plow into something large, the worst that would happen was that they would just sling off the orbit like a flea off a dog's back and then have to backtrack.

Doc was convinced that wasn't going to happen, and he tried to show Fisher the math. Fisher had just nodded like he always did when Doc got into the math on anything concerning orbits and trans-tunnel speeds and finally Doc just stopped and said, "You'll see. It will work."

"Just don't hit the damn planet square on."

"No worries, Skip," he had said.

And that always made Fisher worry. Especially when he called him "Skip" which was short for "Skipper." Doc never did that unless he was worried as well. Fisher got called Skip because he owned *The Lady*, as he called this deep space exploration ship.

Most of the time Doc just called her "The Ship."

They had built her in two years in a huge warehouse on Fisher's parent's estate just north of their hometown, right after they both finally finished with far too many advanced degrees in college.

Fisher had family money in a trust, more than enough, actually, to build a couple ships. And he had patents on a dozen devices he had invented that drew energy from dark matter.

Doc had the idea for the gravity drive that allowed them to not only just float out of a gravity well, but jump long distances very quickly in what Doc called "Trans-Tunnel Flight."

Basically Trans-Tunnel Flight was a form of time-bending warp drive, but when they were in it, space looked like it had become a tunnel, so Doc named it the "Trans-Tunnel Drive."

"Better than Warp Drive," he had said.

In the planning stage, they had decided to make the ship really huge and really cool, right out of a 1950's science fiction movie. They even had painted it silver and put fins like a nifty plane and a pointed nose on it so it looked like a cross between a very fast plane and an old rocket ship. The fins were worthless unless in the atmosphere if the drive went out, and the pointed nose housed nothing but sensors.

They each had huge five-room suites on board, since the ship was the size of a hotel that flew. It was so big, there were parts of this ship Fisher hadn't been in for over a year.

It actually didn't need to be this big, but both of them had figured they never knew what they might run into out in space, or how much room they might need, or who might be riding along.

The actual engine itself took up the size of a small closet and a large warehouse area in a lower deck was filled with many, many spare parts. The rest of the ship had a game room, an exercise room, a small gym, a massive kitchen with a dozen freezers, and numbers of spare bedroom suites for a future crew or guests.

So far, those guest suites had not been used.

Before they took off, they had stocked more food than they would be able to eat in five years, even though from darned-near-anywhere in this area of the galaxy, they could jump back to Earth in a matter of a day or two.

Food was Fisher's passion.

Somewhere back in college, after getting his first doctorate, he had allowed himself to get close to three hundred pounds on his five-foot-ten inch frame. Back then people said he and Doc looked like the old comedy team of Laurel and Hardy, but he was larger back then than Hardy ever got.

And Fisher loved cooking.

And eating.

Especially really rich foods. But a couple doctors told him that if he didn't lose some weight, he was going to have to cut down on many of the dishes he loved to cook if he wanted to live much longer.

He had been only twenty-six when they told him that. It had gotten through.

He had gone exercise crazy.

Right before they left on this trip, he had run in his tenth marathon and he had been training for an Iron Man competition. He now weighed just under one-seventy and that was all muscle. And he could eat anything he damn well wanted.

Somehow, Doc ate everything Fisher served him with relish and never gained a pound and spent only a minor amount of time in the gym, usually when he wanted to talk to Fisher about something and knew Fisher was a captive audience while in an exercise routine.

Fisher didn't feel right if he didn't exercise, just as he didn't feel right when he didn't eat decent food.

One of the most enjoyable aspects of this exploring around space was discovering new types of food and ways of cooking it. He was stockpiling the recipes with hopes of doing a number of cookbooks when they got back home.

He could spend two or three hours a day in the kitchen just testing new foods and writing it all down. And often did.

He doubted anyone would give his books any credit, just as they didn't give his energy inventions even a second look. The power for everything on this ship and Doc's drive came from the energy floating around between matter and dark matter.

For some reason Fisher had the ability to understand when something hidden was between two obvious things.

He had perfected the idea of using the energy between the two states of matter while in school and applied for patents, but no professor would let him write it as a thesis. No one really gave his ideas any credit at all, actually, just as they didn't give Doc's trans-tunnel drive and anti-gravity work anything but laughter.

If they could only see them now.

Finally, Doc had them slowed enough that the orbit they had settled into seemed stable, even though they were still braking.

"Told you it would work," Doc said, smiling at Fisher, his thin face twisted into mostly bright white teeth and wide blue eyes.

Fisher just shook his head and worked his fingers off the armrests of his chair. "Only emergencies," he said as his stomach started to settle.

"Exactly," Doc said, nodding and going back to continuing to brake them into a stable orbit. "At some point I hope to figure out how we can come out of a trans-tunnel without forward speed. It should be possible."

"Make that a priority," Fisher said.

Suddenly the warning lights on Fisher's heads-up panel flashed into a display that would do a Christmas tree proud.

The orbit they had dropped into had them hitting a large orbiting object in about five seconds.

Fisher kicked off Doc's controls and cut the braking, which allowed them to move out higher away from the planet. On his screen their orbit around the planet changed from a nice circular pattern into a big egg-shaped elliptical orbit.

They flashed past what looked like an orbiting station far too fast to get a good look at it.

And far too close for Fisher's stomach to be happy. He had long ago lost the desire for near-misses on anything.

If they had hit that station, they would have put a very, very large hole in it. Their screens would have kept them safe, but the station and everyone on it would have been in trouble, if not killed instantly.

"Wow, good catch, Fisher," Doc said. "Looks like we have a space-faring culture on this planet."

"Great, just great," Fisher said. "Someone to chase us again after we almost destroy their space station."

Doc laughed. "Yeah, we have a way of making an entrance, don't we?"

3

CALLIE FINALLY DECIDED she couldn't just stand there at the edge of the parking lot any more. She needed to move, to do something, to get more information.

"Let's put our packs in the car and check out the lodge," she said.

"No," Jim said, shaking his head.

He had his cell phone to his ear and was shaking his head. "No one is answering. I've got to get to my wife, my kid."

It was Jim's car they had come up in, so Callie actually had nothing to say about him leaving or not. Even though they were her students, they were all three adults.

"I want to go back too," Barb said, her voice barely holding together. She also had a cell phone to her ear. "My parents in Salem are not answering either."

Callie pulled out her phone and tried to call her office. She got her machine, as expected, so the phones were working. She had no family and no one else to call that she could think of off the top of her head.

The three of them stood there for another two minutes trying everyone they could think to dial.

Phones were working.

No one was answering.

That scared Callie more than she wanted to think about. She was fairly certain she didn't want to know how far whatever had caused this had really spread.

And she had no idea what might have caused it. She did know for certain that those bodies in the cave had died almost instantly and without any sort of trauma.

And it had happened at least a day ago, while they were deep in the cave digging.

And she was certain that it had been the fact that they were deep inside the cave that had saved them.

That cave just might save her again.

She was going to stay, even though she had no idea what was happening.

She had come to trust her gut and her gut told her to stay put.

"You two go," she said.

Then she looked Jim directly in the eye. "You drive carefully. If this is widespread, there will be wrecked cars on the road."

He nodded, his face completely pale.

"And you call me from Cave Junction and tell me what you see."

"I will," he said, nodding. "Be careful."

"You too," Callie said.

Barb just nodded and the two of them turned and almost ran for Jim's car.

Callie stood and watched them drive off down the road.

The silence of the mountain came back in strong around her, like a very, very heavy blanket.

The breeze flowing lightly in the trees was the only sound.

Normally she loved the mountains, the timber, the smells of summer pine, and the silence.

Now the silence just worried her more.

And normally she liked being alone, living alone.

Now being alone scared her far more than she wanted to admit.

Ignoring the two bodies she could see, she started off toward the old lodge down the paved road.

The lodge was a rustic three-story hotel built in the 1930s as part of the construction to put people to work during the Depression. It was a place she found stunning and wonderful.

Everything was wood and a huge river-rock fireplace dominated the two-story main lobby. Huge wooden chandeliers hung in the open areas and a wide staircase next to the big wooden front desk led to the upper floors.

It sat perched on the side of a very deep ravine and on the floor below the lobby was a restaurant and café that looked out over that ravine.

In one part of the restaurant it had formal seating, while in another part it looked like an old counter-diner right out of the 1930s. When the Forest Service remodeled the place, they had kept the early look and décor and she had loved the place the first time she stayed in the old lodge a few years back.

In the lodge she found everyone was dead as well.

She spent the next hour keeping her panic in check and slowly working her way through the building, checking every room with a passkey, knocking on every door and calling out before she opened it.

She counted nineteen people in the entire Lodge on all three floors. A couple of cleaning staff, a front desk clerk, two people downstairs in the kitchen, one person slumped over at the counter, and the rest in their rooms.

All dead.

She went back to the lobby and dropped onto a couch.

She couldn't think.

She couldn't even hardly breathe.

Suddenly her phone rang, making her jump and sending the sound echoing in the large open space of the hotel lobby.

She fished it out of her pocket.

"We're in Cave Junction," Jim said. "We had to move some cars and push others out of the way to get down to here."

"Meet anyone?" she asked.

"Everyone is dead."

"You all right?" she asked, knowing the question was stupid.

"No," he said.

"Any sign of anything moving? Helicopters, planes, anything?"

"No," Jim said. "We're going to keep going."

"Carefully," Callie said. "Call me when you get to Eugene."

"I will," Jim said and hung up.

She doubted that he would. At least not for a very long time after finding his wife and daughter dead.

She just hoped that wouldn't happen and this wasn't that widespread.

But her gut told her it was.

And that meant up here on the mountain, she was alone.

Completely alone.

And she was going to be alone for some time to come.

4

AS DOC BROUGHT them around the planet again and worked to match the orbit of the space station, Fisher scanned the planet. It felt a little like scanning his own home world from a low orbit.

Evidence of human activity was everywhere. Large, sprawling cities on all of the major continents. Thousands of roads and smaller cities and towns.

It looked the same, if not almost identical, as many of the Earth-type planets they had visited. Humans had clearly been seeded on every Goldilocks zone planet that they had come to at some point in the distant past. They had run across no aliens, but humans were everywhere.

And he meant everywhere. So many human civilizations, it was startling.

At least in this small area of the Milky Way Galaxy which they had explored.

At last count, they had found over two hundred Earth-like planets and every one of them had either had human life on them at one point, or still did have thriving civilizations.

And not many of them seemed very far beyond or behind Earth's level, as if they had all started at the exact same time in history.

That bothered him a lot and he and Doc had talked about it, but neither one of them could come up with any reason.

Plus even stranger, all the plants on all the planets were the same as well, as were the animals. Dogs, chickens, pigs, cows, deer, everything, all the same. Clearly every planet had had some sort of terra-forming in a distant past before the humans were placed there.

Very, very strange and it had been their main topic of conversation over meals for the first fifty or so planets. Fisher didn't know how he felt knowing that humans were alone in the galaxy, just not all on the same planet.

And he really didn't know how he felt thinking of himself as part of a huge galaxy-wide lab experiment, which it seemed they might be.

But finally, after finding so many civilizations and having no obvious answers present themselves, Fisher and Doc started growing used to the idea.

If growing used to something that was flat impossible was even possible. Fisher assumed it was.

He and Doc didn't talk about it much anymore.

The human civilization on the planet below also seemed to be around Earth's level of growth and expansion.

But as they went around the dark side in their orbit, Fisher noticed one major problem: Nothing was moving.

And the planet was slowly dropping silent and dark.

Only basic recorded sounds were coming from the surface.

In very short order the entire planet would be ghostly silent.

And very, very dark.

"Doc, we have a problem," Fisher said.

"They can't be coming after us already," Doc said, not looking up from his board as he brought *The Lady* up slowly on the orbiting space station. "We missed them, didn't we?"

"No one is coming after us," Fisher said.

"That's good," Doc said, still not looking up. "So what's the problem?"

Fisher's fingers were moving as fast as he could get them to move over his controls to confirm what he feared, doing test and reading after reading.

All the readings came up the same.

Just a day or so ago something had completely wiped out almost every human being down there.

Not all of them, but almost all of them.

"They are dead," Fisher said, sitting back in his chair and forcing himself to take deep breaths.

"Who's dead," Doc asked.

"Just about everyone on the planet," Fisher said.

At that, Doc looked up.

5

CALLIE SAT ON the big overstuffed couch in the grand foyer of the old lodge for two hours after talking with Jim, just thinking.

One moment she felt so panicked, she wanted to just run, get into a car and drive. The next moment she would feel calm, working on a plan of survival until someone came.

The survival plan eventually won over the panic. But not by much.

She did a quick calculation.

It had to be Thursday morning, around eleven. From her best calculations of what she saw of the bodies in the cave and in the lodge here, everyone had been dead for just over twenty-four hours.

And if she was right on that, she knew that she was going to have to move fast if she was going to have a sane and comfortable place to stay here in the lodge.

When in college the first time, she had started as pre-med and one of the things they forced the students to do near the end of the first year was actually smell a human body that had been rotting for a couple of days.

It was not an odor anyone could forget. And that day she had taken three showers and still didn't feel like she had the smell off her. That smell, along with a few other events, most notably an old boyfriend also planning on going on to the same medical school, convinced her to move to a major in paleontology, which she ended up loving with far more of a passion than she could have ever imagined.

She loved puzzles, finding clues to history where no one else would think to look. And now she could never imagine herself as a medical doctor.

But she knew, without a doubt, that she needed to deal with the bodies inside the lodge if she hoped to stay here until things started to clear up. And since Jim had reported the deaths were as far as Cave Junction, down in the valley below this lodge, she really had nowhere better to go.

In the basement she had seen a large four-wheeled supply cart for bringing in supplies to the kitchen from the driveway outside. It was low to the ground and on four solid wheels. She decided she would use that.

She borrowed some clothes, including a large yellow maintenance jacket, some gloves, and some snow pants from a maintenance storage area. There she also found two large generators set up to take over when the power went down.

She patted one on the side, very happy to see them.

Then, with a surgical mask on, the heavy coat, the gloves, and the snow pants, she went to work moving the bodies.

She started in the basement kitchen area since she was going to need that area to cook and for supplies. She managed to get one body up and on the cart and wheeled out the supply door and into the driveway before she suddenly questioned what she was going to do with the poor people she was moving.

The day was starting to heat up and that meant that the smell would get worse quickly.

The woman on the cart was about fifty, had a wedding ring on one finger, and a hairnet on graying hair. She wore what looked to be a blue and white restaurant uniform.

Callie had taken her keys, but put the woman's purse and coat with her, in case down the road someone would need to identify the remains.

But now, standing outside in the late afternoon air, Callie realized she had a real problem.

This was more than a body on the cart, this had been a person and Callie just couldn't dump her out onto the road for the animals to tear apart.

She had to treat these people with respect, at least as much as she could under these circumstance. But where could she put everyone that animals couldn't get into and that she would have enough energy to move them to?

She knew that up near the parking lot was an old dormitory where the park rangers lived, but that would be too far for her to push the cart up that much hill.

She left the woman and the cart near the kitchen entrance and started up the shallow-sloped driveway toward the main road.

About halfway up she saw a medium-sized supply truck parked to one side of the lodge, tucked into a parking spot like it was going to be there for the night.

The back of the truck was mostly empty except for some cases of canned fruits, which Callie quickly unloaded onto the ground in a shady spot beside the building. She would take those inside later.

Then she climbed in behind the steering wheel of the truck.

She had driven her share of large trucks on different archeological digs over the years, especially when she was a graduate student.

She didn't expect the keys to be in the ignition, or on top of the visor, but she checked both places. Then she checked the closed tray beside the driver's seat. The keys were in there, along with a couple of Snicker's Bars.

One bar she put in the jacket pocket, the other she took a big bite out of, realizing she hadn't eaten since an an hour inside the cave. The wonderful nuts and chocolate tasted great, far better than it should have.

She was going to have to be careful to watch her food and when she ate. She often had a habit of forgetting to eat when she was busy.

Or stressed.

She managed to get the truck backed down the loading area and fairly close to the door into the supply area of the kitchen without hitting anything.

Shutting off the engine, she again noticed the silence of the mountains around her.

She went around to the back of the truck and quickly figured out how to lower the loading lift. She got the cart with the woman on the tailgate lift and up and into the truck.

Callie rolled her off the cart and apologized, then laid her on her back, her hands on her chest, near the back wall.

Then Callie went back for another poor soul who had been caught in whatever had happened to everyone.

In one hour she had everyone out of the basement and kitchen and maintenance area and into the truck.

One floor clear.

She was sweating like crazy and decided to stop for a quick bite of lunch and a large bottle of water.

She stripped off the big orange coat and the gloves and mask, letting the cool evening air take some of the sweat away. She exercised every day and had never been afraid of hard labor, but this was more than she had expected it to be. Dead human bodies were difficult to move around.

And they were all starting to smell.

She washed off her hands and face and blew out her nose, then went to work finding something to eat, even though she was far, far from hungry.

She forced herself to eat a turkey sandwich and an apple while sitting at the old counter in the silence, watching the afternoon slowly pass on the mountains around her through the big windows.

She felt incredibly alone, but she wouldn't let herself think about what she was doing.

Or even try to guess at what had happened.

There would be more than enough time for that later. Right now she just had to act.

She ate the second Snicker's Bar for dessert, then she put her protective clothes back on and took the cart up the elevator like she was a bellman from hell and started to retrieve the dead bodies from the main floor, starting with the poor woman behind the desk.

It was going to be a long, long afternoon and evening.

6

THEY DID TEN ORBITS over the next few hours, recording and studying everything they could.

To Fisher there was no doubt the planet below had just gone through something horrible. Actually, the planet was fine, but vast numbers of the humans and a bunch of animal life had died very, very suddenly.

And very recently.

Maybe just a day ago, at most.

There were numbers of smaller animals and some larger ones still alive, and human bodies lay everywhere, in every building, on every street.

Not one corner of the planet had been spared.

There were fires in most every major city, but all were minor. There seemed to have been no violence in the slightest.

Fisher felt really, really bad for the people who had somehow survived. He couldn't imagine what they were going through, finding loved ones dead, walking around among the bodies.

It made his stomach ache just thinking about it.

Something had killed a couple billion people on the planet and had done it quickly, where they stood, as they walked, as they drove cars that looked to Fisher frighteningly like cars from home.

"You got any idea how many are alive down there?" Fisher finally asked Doc.

"Not a clue," Doc said, his voice unnaturally soft. "Not that many compared to how many died."

He looked over, his eyes looking haunted. They had run into a couple of Earth-like planets with no humans and only signs of a civilization in the distant past. That was one thing, almost a scientific curiosity as to what happened.

Humans did have a way of killing each other and a few planets hadn't escaped that.

But it was a different thing when they could see human bodies littering the streets and filling the buildings.

Recently dead human bodies.

Millions and millions and millions of them.

A vastly different thing.

And what worried Fisher more than anything else was that this could happen to their home world. They somehow needed to find out what happened here.

They sat in silence until finally Fisher had an idea.

"The station," Fisher said.

Doc nodded. After this many years together, they often didn't have to finish sentences or thoughts.

They both knew that the instruments there might give them some sort of understanding of what had killed most of the human population of this planet.

Doc's fingers again flew over the control board, bringing them even closer in to match the orbit of the large space station.

Fisher just felt stunned. He was not really looking forward to going into that station. More than likely it was full of dead bodies as well.

They would have to be very, very careful.

Suddenly space around the planet filled with numbers of huge spaceships.

It looked like at least fifty, maybe more from what Fisher could tell.

They just appeared out of nowhere and at a dead stop, spaced evenly around the planet.

From what Fisher could tell, they made *The Lady* look like a kid's ship in a bathtub compared to an aircraft carrier.

"What the…" Fisher said, pushing back in his chair as if he needed to get farther away from those clearly alien monster ships.

Doc glanced up and jerked, also pushing back.

Then suddenly, on the sensors, Fisher started reading humans disappearing from the planet below.

Some alone, some scattered in groups.

But if the big ships were taking them, they weren't missing anyone.

One moment a person was on the planet, the next they were gone.

Fisher did a quick calculation. If those ships were as big as they seemed, there were enough ships to handle all the survivors from below.

Fisher pointed to the readings and tapped Doc who glanced at it and nodded.

"They are transporting humans to the ships," he said. "Looks like we found our seeders."

"We are not the originals," a voice said clearly inside the control room of *The Lady*. Only it wasn't Fisher's voice or Doc's.

And it was in perfect English.

Then everything around them shimmered for a moment and stabilized again.

The Lady was no longer floating in space near an empty space station. It was now seemingly sitting on a huge landing dock inside another ship.

"Oh, man," Fisher said, trying to keep the last bit of control he had. Somehow he managed to not scream and run to the back of the ship, which would have done no good at all, but he was sure it would have felt better than just sitting there.

"Now what are we going to do?" he finally asked his partner as they stared out the viewport at what appeared to be the inside of a huge hanger deck.

Doc shook his head slowly, clearly as shaken as Fisher had ever seen him before.

Then Doc turned and with a half-smile and shrug said, "Go and say hello?"

Fisher preferred the idea of running and screaming much better, but figured Doc was more than likely right.

7

BY EARLY EVENING, Callie had cleared the main floor, taking the bodies down the service elevator and out onto the truck.

After the sun went down, she had started closing the door to the truck just to make sure no animals got in. She was far from used to the smell and it clearly wasn't getting any better.

There were six bodies on the top floor in four rooms. She needed to get them out before she could stop.

Two couples and two single guests. Or at least guests who were alone when the death hit, as she was starting to think of it.

She didn't know what else to call what had happened besides "the death."

Over the next hour she got four of them out, the one couple together. Now she only had one more couple, but she wasn't looking forward to this at all, which was why Callie had left them to last.

The couple had been young, very young, and when the death hit, they had been making love. So both were nude and even though they were dead, Callie felt embarrassed she had to see them and touch them and move them from that position.

When she found them the first time, she had covered them with a blanket.

Now she had no choice. She had to get them out of the hotel.

"Think like a doctor," she said to herself as she opened their door, the rancid smell hitting her solidly. "You've seen naked flesh before. You can do this."

She pushed the cart over beside the bed, then pushed back the blanket.

The young girl, a natural redhead, was slumped on top of the boy who didn't look much older than eighteen.

She pulled the girl over toward the cart. For a moment Callie didn't think the girl was going to let go of her boyfriend.

Then she did and flopped down on the cart, her dead eyes staring up at the ceiling.

Callie then took the boy and rolled him over on top of his girl-friend on the cart.

Again, they looked like they were making love.

Callie quickly threw a blanket over them and somehow managed to get them downstairs and into the truck. She left them together, covered in a blanket and threw a change of clothes and their inden-tifications in beside them.

Then, as she closed the back of the truck, Callie said simply to all nineteen in there, "Rest in peace."

She moved the truck up to the parking lot and parked it near the two bodies there. Animals had done horrid work to those two and she didn't even want to try to load them into the truck. There was only so much she could do and she was beyond tired.

She took off the orange coat and draped it over the woman on the ground, then took off the ski pants and draped them over the man.

That wouldn't help them, but it was the best she could do.

She could do nothing for those in the cave.

Then suddenly it dawned on her that Dave was still in there with his dead wife.

She had completely and totally forgotten about him.

Suddenly her heart was racing and she was excited again. She had someone to help her survive all this.

How could she have forgotten him?

She took a flashlight she had been carrying and a second one from out of the glove box in the truck, then headed down the path through the dark trees to the mouth of the cave.

The smell in the cave was bad, but she waded in.

"Dave!"

Her words echoed among the rocks.

Dave was still with his wife, her head cradled in his lap.

At first Callie thought he was just sleeping, hunched over her. But as she got closer, she knew that wasn't the case.

A large knife lay beside Dave and there was a dark pool of dried blood on the asphalt.

Dave had slashed his wrists and died there with his wife, not willing to leave her.

"Damn it all to hell," she said, resisting the urge to just kick his body. "I needed your help you selfish bastard."

Then she managed to get herself a little under control.

"Sorry, Dave," she said, her voice soft. "I've just seen so much death already, I didn't need more."

She stared at the guide she had come to like over the last few days.

"Rest in peace," she said. "All of you."

Then she turned and headed back to the lodge.

She needed the longest, hottest shower she had ever taken with as much soap and shampoo that she could find.

And then she needed some sleep.

And maybe, just maybe, she might wake up from this nightmare.

8

BOTH FISHER AND DOC did some quick checking and the atmosphere outside the ship in the huge space dock was normal, no bad things in it that could kill them. And the gravity seemed to be Earth-normal as well.

Beyond that, they couldn't tell much of anything about the ship around them past what they could see in the huge room. The dock had to be as large as a football stadium and could have easily held three or four ships *The Lady's* size.

They tested, but every control they had was locked down solid and the engines were offline. Something was blocking them. They were going nowhere under their own power.

"You ready, Skip?" Doc asked, pretending to stretch like he was relaxed about meeting the owners of these huge ships.

Fisher just shook his head and stood. "Seems like we have no choice, doesn't it?"

A good minute later they were standing on the deck looking around. The sides of the room seem to vanish in the distance and Fisher had been clearly wrong. This room could hold twenty ships the size of theirs, and have room between them all.

And he thought they had built a large ship when they built *The Lady*. Everything in space was relative it seemed.

Then, just as the first time they were grabbed, everything shimmered and they found themselves in a high-ceilinged meeting room with tables full of meats and vegetables and breads along one wall. It looked like preparations for a huge party, but so far the guests hadn't arrived.

To Fisher, the place had a warm feel and it seemed that someone was pumping in the smell of baking bread as well. Or maybe they actually were baking bread nearby.

He turned slowly around, surveying the large meeting room. There were stacks of blankets and chairs and cots everywhere. One wall was filled with a huge viewport that looked down on the greens and blues and whites of the planet below.

"Looks like we are just in time for the party," Doc said.

"If you had come to this planet a day earlier," a voice said from behind them, "you more than likely would have been as dead as most of those on the planet below."

Fisher and Doc spun around to see a man about Fisher's height and weight walking toward them, smiling. He had gray/silver hair, wore jeans and a green short-sleeved shirt tucked into his pants. He looked as normal and as human as anyone from Earth.

And as far as Fisher could tell, he was speaking perfect English.

They had met a few human cultures that had perfected some sort of translation devices that just made it sound like they were speaking English. But this was even more advanced. His lips seemed to match what he was saying.

Considering the size of this ship they were in, Fisher figured he would have been less stunned if an alien had joined them spouting six arms and a beak and squeaking their national anthem.

The guy extended his hand for Fisher to shake. "I'm Benson."

"Fisher," he said, carefully shaking Benson's hand.

It felt as normal as any human handshake, which bothered Fisher even more.

"Doc," said softly as he shook Benson's hand next.

"So you are the two explorers we've been hearing about," Benson said, smiling. "I understand you have had some adventures."

"A few," Fisher said, even more shocked that anyone had followed them around this area of space. Granted, it was a tiny area in comparison to the entire Milky Way Galaxy, but they had still covered a lot of light years and visited a few hundred Earth-like planets. And tracking them through open trans-tunnel space wasn't like following footprints in the mud. Or at least Fisher didn't think it was.

"So where are you two from?" Benson asked.

"Earth."

Fisher gave him the answer he knew would make the guy smile and at the same time give him no information at all, since most of the human planets they had visited had called their planets Earth. In fact, every one of them had.

He did smile. "I don't blame you for not wanting to tell me. How about I show you around and tell you what we are doing and then maybe you'll feel more like talking. And maybe you can help us a little with what's coming. We're going to need all the help we can get for a few hours." He waved at the room that was prepared for visitors.

"I find it fascinating," he said as he started to lead them toward a door, "that a human culture in this area has advanced as far as you have."

Fisher almost told him that the rest of their planet hadn't just yet, but instead just nodded and said, "Hold on a second. Can you tell us what happened down there? And what's happening now? How come all those people are vanishing off the surface?"

Fisher pointed at the planet that could be seen out of a large viewport on one side of the room.

Benson tapped something on his wrist and in the air near them an image of the Milky Way Galaxy came into being, spinning in the air.

Impressive three-dimensional image.

Then like focusing in, the view shifted down to this spiral arm of the galaxy and then to this small section of space. There had to be five hundred suns represented by nothing more than bright colored lights floating in the air.

One light was suddenly circled in the air by a red ring.

"An explosion in this sun caused rays of extreme electro-magnetic energy to be sent out into space."

From the circled star a number of white rays seemed to expand outward.

Benson went on. "By the time we noticed the explosion and calculated the frequency of the energy and then traced its path, we were too late to get here to save all the people of this planet. We couldn't mount a big enough rescue force to even attempt it."

Fisher was watching and it was clear Benson was very, very upset at that fact.

"EMP blast killed them where they stood," Doc said, nodding. "That makes sense now. The right frequency would short-circuit human brains like that."

Benson nodded. "About two million of the population survived by accidentally being in different forms of shelters or underground or inside something that shielded them. They didn't know it was coming."

Then Fisher finally understood what we had seen and why they were taking people off the planet. "But there is a second blast of energy following the first."

Benson nodded. "You guessed it. We got here ahead of that with a large enough fleet to get all the survivors out of the way. What you are witnessing is my people taking them off the planet during the night hours in each area of the planet. This ship should start loading in an hour. We will move out of the way of the wave for a few hours, then come back and return everyone."

"We arrived between the waves?" Doc asked.

"About one day after the first one," Benson said. "And about ten hours ahead of the second. Your shielding might have sheltered you from the second one since it's not as powerful, but it might not have either. Before you leave we will help you strengthen that shielding some for the future."

Fisher looked at Benson and then nodded. "Thanks."

"So you go around rescuing planets full of humans?" Doc asked.

Benson shook his head sadly. "First time. But after this we will be more vigilant. Billions died down there before we got here."

He seemed actually deeply affected by that, so Fisher tried to change the subject.

"So you know who seeded humans on so many planets in this area of the galaxy?" he asked.

"In every area of the galaxy," Benson said so matter-of-factly that it bothered Fisher. "There are hundreds and hundreds of thousands of human civilizations in different stages of development in this galaxy. And no one knows much about the people or race who did it except that it took them over fifty thousand years to complete the task for the entire galaxy."

"Your planet was seeded as well?" Doc asked. "How come you are more advanced than any culture we have seen?"

"We were all seeded," Benson said, nodding. Again the floating map of the Milky Way Galaxy came into being in the air beside them. "My home planet is there, also called Earth."

A circle appeared around a dot a third of the way around the galaxy. Then another appeared around a dot Fisher knew to be the sun they were orbiting.

"We are here at the moment," Benson said. "My area of the galaxy was seemingly seeded first, so civilizations that survived in that area are the most advanced. This arm of the galaxy was next, and as you move around in a clockwise direction, each human civilization gets more primitive."

"Wow," was all Fisher could think to say. Stunned didn't begin to describe how he felt.

Benson went on. "Our area of the galaxy has formed a large organization of aligned planets and about fifty worlds work together. That's why we could mount such a large fleet on such short notice."

"And no alien life at all?" Doc asked.

"Nothing above basic animal level," Benson said. "The Seeders, as we call them, not only seeded humans, but all the plant and animal life it would take to sustain human civilizations in the growth years."

"All the same on every planet?" Doc asked.

"All the same," Benson said. "Exactly."

Fisher stood there shaking his head and just staring at the image of the galaxy floating in the empty meeting room air. He remembered how stunned he had felt every time they came across another human civilization during their first year exploring. But after a while he had just come to expect it.

Now he was feeling that same feeling again. It was just too much to grasp.

Humans always thought they were alone in the galaxy. It seemed they were. But not in the way people back home might think.

Finally he shook his head and glanced at Benson, who looked almost haunted as he stared out the viewport at the planet below. For some reason he clearly felt responsible for all those deaths.

Fisher decided that their only hope in learning even more from Benson and his people was to confide in him.

"Could you focus this image in again to this area of space?" Fisher asked, pointing to the floating galaxy.

Benson nodded and the floating image focused down and Fisher pointed to a yellow star about sixty light years from this sun. "That's our Earth. And we are the only two that have this kind of technology at the moment."

Benson nodded. "I figured as much," he said. "On a couple of the planets in our area single explorers were the first out between the stars as well."

"So we are the first in this area of space?" Doc asked.

Benson nodded. "But after some of your visits to a few of the planets, I have a hunch those won't be far behind now that they know it's possible."

How in the world had he traced us? Fisher was about to ask, but Doc got a question in first.

"So is your drive the same technology as ours?" Doc asked as Fisher turned to stare back out at the damaged planet below.

Out of the corner of his eye he saw Benson shrug. "Just more advanced, but the same principles. If you want, I'll get some of our scientists to explain some of it to you."

"You'd do that?" Fisher asked, turning to Benson. Fisher was again as stunned as Doc looked.

"Why not?" Benson asked. "We're all out here together. If we can't help other human civilizations, what's the point?"

Doc opened his mouth, but nothing came out. He was like a kid that had just been offered everything for free in a candy store.

Fisher just shook his head and turned back to the viewport. "So how do we help all those people still down there?"

"When they get here, we just keep them comfortable and calmed down as much as possible," Benson said. "After we put them back, we can't do much. At least not right now. Not until they get through the rebuilding stage, which the experts tell me is going to take a few hundred years at least."

"They have enough population to survive?" Fisher asked, surprised.

Benson nodded. "More than enough. The Seeders only put a hundred and forty-four thousand humans on every planet and all but a few populations managed to keep going. There's almost two million alive down there still."

That exact number the Seeders used bothered Fisher, but now was not the time to ask. A lot about this was bothering him, but he knew he was in such shock, nothing was fitting together.

"You are saving millions of humans," Doc said. "That's impressive."

"And we didn't save many millions and millions more," Benson said, his voice soft. "But the one thing we know about humans, we survive. And the people of this planet will as well. The Seeders made sure we all had that trait."

CALLIE MADE IT BACK to the lodge and turned on lights in the big lobby, then locked all the doors to the place. She wasn't sure exactly who she was locking doors to stay safe from, but she felt better doing that.

At this point, she was too tired to question anything she was doing. She just had to keep moving, stumbling forward.

The only clothes she had were the ones she wore in the cave and they were all muddy. So she headed back up to the room where the young couple had stayed and borrowed the woman's suitcase that had been tucked off in a corner of a second room, so the smell had not yet got to it. The young woman had seemed to be about the same size as Callie.

Callie went down to the main floor, found the biggest suite on the floor. The suite had been made up for some future guest that would now clearly not arrive.

Callie left the clothes that she had been wearing out in the hall near another door, then went back, locked the suite door and turned on the shower.

She could feel that she was completely numb. She had just been moving, not thinking, and now she was so tired, she didn't dare allow herself to think about anything.

After a long hot shower, she got her hair dry with the blow dryer, then went through the girl's suitcase.

Callie found a nice pair of sweat pants and some new underwear that the girl had never worn that fit Callie fine.

She also had a green and white University of Oregon sweatshirt, so Callie put that on as well, along with some nice new socks. Clearly, this trip with her boyfriend to this lodge had been something special for the young girl.

Then in the sweatshirt and sweatpants and socks, Callie crawled into the big featherbed.

She almost shut off the light, but then on second thought decided she wasn't ready to face darkness at the moment.

She curled up under the large comforter on the soft old bed and was instantly asleep.

What seemed like only a moment later she was awakened by the strangest feeling of floating.

Another moment later she found herself in a bright room with hundreds of other people. She wasn't laying down, but instead standing.

All of the people she faced looked shocked.

As shocked as she was feeling.

If this was a dream, it was the strangest and most real dream she had ever had.

Some of the people around her started crying, some dropped to the floor and huddled with their heads down.

Everyone looked like they had been through a very, very hard day.

Some were dressed, some were naked and others were moving to cover the naked ones in blankets.

And the distinct smell of human death seemed to suddenly be everywhere again.

Callie looked around. Huge tables of food filled one wall, medical staff seemed to be working their way through the people, while still other rescuers were helping others toward what looked like showers.

She scanned the room until suddenly what was behind her caught her eye.

She spun around, only to be faced with the most incredible sight she had ever seen.

An entire wall that looked like a window and seemed like a lot of movies she had seen shot from orbit.

Below her the Earth was slowly spinning past.

Not possible.

That view was too much for her to take.

She could feel the room growing faint and she started to slump to the ground, but strong hands caught her.

She mumbled "Thanks" before everything went black.

10

FISHER STOOD AND WATCHED the people appear in the big room.

It was just creepy. One moment there would be an empty spot, the next moment a person would be standing there. No shimmering, no sound, nothing. Just sort of "blink" and a person appeared.

Creepy.

Benson had left them almost an hour before to tend to other duties, so Fisher and Doc had stayed in the room, gotten a quick sandwich, then helped the crew get ready for survivors to come in.

A guy by the name of Glove explained to them what was going to happen. It seemed they were going to bring in about two hundred survivors to this room, give them medical attention, let them get cleaned up and eat something and try to just keep them calm for a number of hours until they could be returned to the exact spot where they were taken.

"Will the rescued people remember any of this?" Doc had asked.

Grove had shaken his head. "Very few of them will, and those few who do will think they just had a very strange dream."

Grove had stationed all the help around the room to assist people as they appeared. He told Fisher and Doc that when the room was full, all the survivors that were coming to this room were here, Benson would come and give an explanation of what was happening.

Then it would be up to the staff of the room to keep the people calm and fed until they could be sent back.

Fisher had been assigned an area near the big window looking over the city.

At first he was stunned at the smell of a few people as they arrived. The worst-smelling were taken out of the room almost at once, which Fisher appreciated. He had been around dead animal bodies before, but never anything like this.

After fifteen minutes, most of the people had arrived. He had helped a couple people find chairs and reassured a couple others that a full explanation would be coming.

Then, when he thought the room couldn't hold any more, about ten feet to his left a beautiful woman appeared, looking as stunned as everyone else.

Fisher had to step back. The attraction to her was so intense, he could feel it instantly.

She was the most beautiful woman he could remember seeing.
Ever.

And he wasn't honestly the type that noticed attractive women. He had been so wrapped up in his work and studies for years and years, a relationship hadn't even crossed his mind.

It just seemed like it would have been too much work and taken too much time.

And back when he was fat, no woman would look at him anyway.

So the fact that he had a reaction to a woman was very different for him.

Very, very different.

His heart was racing, he felt short of breath, and all he could do was stare at her.

She looked to be just slightly shorter than he was and about the same age. She had short brown hair that was messed up so that it looked like she had been sleeping when brought up to the ship.

She wore a green and yellow sweatshirt that looked like it was from a university somewhere and dark sweatpants. She didn't have shoes on, only green socks.

And she looked to be in great shape, as if she exercised.

She stood there, alone, sort of staring around, taking in the big room and clearly trying to get her balance and bearings.

And then suddenly she caught sight of the view out the big window behind her.

She spun around to stare at it.

Fisher somehow got himself to move and just in time as she stared at the planet below and then just sort of slowly started to slump.

He managed to catch her before she hit the floor.

She mumbled something and then passed out.

He picked her up, savoring the feel of her in his arms. He quickly moved her over to an empty chair where he eased her down into place.

Fisher got her situated and motioned for one of the big ship's medical staff.

An older woman in a white smock came quickly over and knelt in front of the woman he had caught.

The medical person did a quick check with a small medical device and scanner and nodded. "Exhaustion, hunger, and shock," she said. "She'll be fine. Stay with her. I'll have someone bring some food and something to drink."

Fisher nodded and pulled another chair over facing the woman he found so attractive.

A juice drink and a few cookies were brought over from the food table by another staff member and handed to Fisher just as the woman started to come around.

"You're going to be all right," Fisher said softly.

He wanted to lean in and touch her hand, but instead stayed back.

The woman opened her eyes and seemed to take a moment before she focused on Fisher's smiling face.

At least he was doing his best to smile. His stomach was twisting and he was scared to death even trying to take care of this woman.

When her eyes focused, she jerked back in her chair.

"Sorry," he said, still smiling. "I'm really not a monster. Honest. A scientist, yes, but not a monster."

She didn't respond to his lame attempt at a joke, but he kept smiling. Damned if he could think of anything else to do.

"I..." she tried to say, but nothing came out.

"Here, drink a little of this," he said, indicating the glass. "I have no idea what it is, but more than likely some sort of apple juice."

She nodded and tried to take the glass in her shaking hands.

Fisher just held onto it and she closed her hands around his to guide it to her mouth.

He thought his heart was going to leap out of his body.

Her touch was wonderful, her skin slightly rough, but still electrical.

She just kept staring at him, into his eyes, and he helped her take a drink.

After a little sip she nodded. "Apple."

"Good to know," he said, still smiling like he was a fool in a carnival.

He pulled the glass away, suddenly very disappointed he was not touching her hands again.

He then offered her a cookie.

"Again, I have no idea what kind, but the medical people said you should eat them. They said that more than likely you were hungry and in shock."

She nodded, took the cookie and pretty much devoured it.

"Peanut butter," she said as he handed her another.

"Good to know."

She glanced back at the view of the planet below, then back at Fisher. "Is that real?"

Fisher nodded. "You are in orbit above the planet. A very nice man is going to show up in a few minutes and try to explain this all."

"Were you down there as well?" she asked.

He shook his head. "I just arrived above your planet about four hours ago."

"Arrived?" she asked. "Where exactly are you from?"

Fisher had no way to not tell this incredibly attractive woman anything but the truth.

He pointed off to his right. "About sixty some light years in that direction."

All she could do was nod as she worked on the other cookie and alternated her attention from looking into his eyes to staring at the planet below.

CALLIE SLOWLY CAME BACK from the darkness.

Before she opened her eyes she heard the sounds of a large room of people, some crying, some talking, but all the voices sort of merging into one loud sound.

She had spun around and looked out from what seemed to be a position in orbit. The moment before, she had been asleep in a lodge in Oregon after cleaning out more dead bodies than she wanted to think about.

The quick turn had made her dizzy, more than likely made worse by being suddenly woken up.

That lodge had been a nightmare she hoped she would wake up from.

But she didn't expect to wake up in yet another unexplained nightmare and then just pass out like a real baby. That was not like her at all.

She was now sitting in a chair and she slowly eased her eyes open.

Someone was sitting across from her, but she let the last of the dizziness fade a little more before she tried to focus on that person.

When her eyes did focus, she jerked back.

She was facing the most handsome man she had ever seen, with the most beautiful, if not strained smile on his face.

He had short brown hair, bright green eyes, was clean-shaven, and had shoulders like an athlete. She guessed him to be about her age.

He made a lame sort of joke about not being a monster and not meaning to scare her.

He hadn't scared her. She just hadn't expected to wake up to her perfect man. Now if the guy had a brain, she would be in heaven.

Then she looked around, realizing she actually hadn't dreamed being on a ship in orbit.

Mr. Handsome offered her a juice he thought might be apple juice and then had to help her drink it.

His hands felt wonderful.

Hers were shaking.

He said something about her being in shock, being exhausted, and being hungry.

Of course. She really needed to learn to pay attention to her eating. She had only had a sandwich six or so hours before crawling in bed after doing all that physical work moving the bodies.

No wonder she passed out.

The apple juice tasted wonderful and then he gave her a peanut butter cookie she managed to not completely inhale.

She could feel her nerves starting to calm as the juice and cookie hit her system.

She just kept staring into the guy's wonderful green eyes, not at all really wanting to look away. But then finally she did, turning to look out at the planet below them.

Then she asked him if he had been down there and he had said he hadn't been, that he had just arrived, and was from a planet about sixty light years away.

Okay, she was still dreaming.

But at least now instead of dreaming about moving dead people, she was dreaming about the most handsome man she had ever met.

Then, as Mr. Handsome had promised, a man came out of a back room and got up onto a stage.

Somehow he managed to get everyone's attention. Mr. Handsome moved his chair around so that he would also face the guy talking. She felt disappointed because she couldn't look into his eyes anymore.

She finished off the second cookie, downed the last of the apple juice, and he gave her a third cookie.

She was feeling a lot better.

"My name is Benson," the man said, smiling at the room that Callie guessed had at least two or three hundred people in it, if not more.

"And this is my ship you are on. We are in orbit around your planet. There are just under one hundred other ships similar in size and shape to this one also here representing almost fifty different planets in this rescue operation."

There was a lot of murmuring and Callie understood why. That simple information was almost too much for anyone to swallow.

Benson held up his hand. "All of us are as human as all of you, I can promise you that. And we are here to help."

The sounds in the room slowly settled away and she glanced at Mr. Handsome, who seemed to be very intently interested in what Benson was saying, as if he had never heard it before.

"About a day ago your planet was hit by an intense wave of electromagnetic energy."

On a large screen behind him the image of this area of the galaxy appeared and showed one star sending out an intense white beam of light and it intersected another sun.

"The electromagnetic pulse basically short-circuited the human brain. You were all saved in one way or another because you were either inside something that sheltered you, or underground. Just over two million survived the first pulse."

"First pulse?" someone shouted.

Callie didn't much like the idea of a second pulse either.

"That's right, a weaker but still deadly second pulse will be hitting your planet in just under five hours. We will have everyone off the planet when that happens and a safe distance away."

"Then what happens?" someone shouted.

"Then we bring you back to your home and let you begin the process of rebuilding your world. The trip away and back will take a very short amount of time, so rest, eat, and let our staff help you in any way they can. The crew in this room came a long ways for this moment to help you all survive."

"You are actually going to rescue all two million survivors?" someone shouted from the other side of the room before Benson had a chance to turn away from the microphone.

"Every last person," Benson said, with an intensity that surprised Callie.

Then he turned and left the stage and the room.

Around her the noise exploded as everyone tried to talk at once.

Mr. Handsome scooted his chair around so he could again face her.

All she could do was stare into those fantastic green eyes and try, try, try to get one simple thought together.

Nothing.

12

CALLIE FINALLY FELT like she was getting some of her brain back.

"Would you like something more to eat?" the handsome man across from her asked. He didn't seem to be inclined to leave her and for that she felt very grateful.

"I would," she said. "Thank you."

He stood and started to turn toward the food when she asked, "What's your name?"

"Fisher," he said, smiling at her. "And yours?"

"Callie," she said.

"Right back with some food. I could use some myself."

She sat and watched him walk away. She liked his name and was stunned at how attracted she was to him in these strange circumstances.

But she was. And she couldn't stop staring at his butt. Clearly he had the walk of someone who knew how to carry himself. An athlete.

And he filled out those jeans perfectly.

And his broad shoulders moved with an ease she had not seen before.

When he vanished in the crowd, she turned and let herself just stare out at the planet below, not wanting to pay any attention to the others in the room. Interestingly enough, the view of the planet below calmed her.

She forced herself to take deep breaths and relax some.

What seemed like only a moment later he brought her back a plastic plate with a sandwich made on white bread, an apple, and five more cookies.

He had a plate as well that had a matching sandwich and cookies.

He also had two plastic bottles of what looked to be some sort of juice that looked like what she had before.

"They tell me this is apple juice again," he said, handing her a bottle. "And the sandwich is turkey."

Callie just looked at her plate, shaking her head. "How is it that alien people from other planets can get this kind of food?"

"You wouldn't believe me if I told you," he said, shaking his head and taking a bite of the cookie first.

"Try me," she said. "At this point I'll believe darned near anything."

He laughed and she loved the sound of his laugh. "I hear you there," he said. "I can't believe I'm sitting here either."

Then he waved his hand. "Sorry, got way off track with that. Let me try to answer your question, but remember I warned you that you wouldn't believe me."

She laughed and motioned for him to go ahead as she took a bite of the wonderful-tasting turkey sandwich on the soft white bread. It was salted just perfectly and had some sort of light sauce that gave it just the right flavor.

"Well," he said, "from what I have seen, and have been told, a race called The Seeders terra-formed every possible planet in the galaxy and planted the exact same plants and humans. So every planet has human civilizations and eat basically the same things."

Callie just looked at him. She could tell he was serious.

She shook her head. "You are right, I don't believe you."

He laughed. "Oh, trust me, unless I had seen all this for myself, I wouldn't have believed it either. I sometimes still don't."

"So exactly what are you doing here?" she asked.

He pointed to a tall, thin, nerdy-looking guy standing talking with a group of people near the viewport. "That's my friend, Doc. We're both from the same place and we invented a ship that could take us out into interstellar space."

"Something like this ship?" she asked.

He laughed. "Oh, heavens no. Our ship, *The Lady*, is sitting like a tiny flea in this ship's docking port. We thought our ship was huge when we built it. Guess not, huh?"

She nodded, so he went on.

"We had visited a few hundred planets like yours, almost all with thriving human civilizations at about the same level as yours and mine. Not kidding. We just got to this system about five hours ago and were trying to figure out what had happened when all these big ships suddenly arrived and started pulling off survivors from below."

"So they rescued you as well?" she asked.

"Sort of," he said. "They tell us our shields on *The Lady* might have saved us from the second wave. But they wanted the extra help here and we were more than glad enough to help. Seems these people are really into helping other races and sharing information."

"Sure seems that way," Callie said. "Where are they from?"

"From what I'm told, about fifty planets in a sector of the galaxy that was seeded earlier, so they are more advanced than this area of space, than your people and mine."

She just shook her head. "So if we're all from different planets, how come we can all speak the same language?"

"Now that's something that's been bothering me as well," he said. "I just haven't had the chance to ask anyone how that works."

She took another bite of the sandwich and then opened the juice.

"I hope I'm not being too personal," he said, looking worried, "but did you have family down there and how did you survive?"

"No family," she said. "And I'm a paleontologist and a professor. I was on a dig in a regional cave."

"Your students survive as well?" he asked.

Suddenly her brain clicked in even more. "They did, at least as long as they were with me. We didn't come out of the cave until this morning to discover what had happened. They had family and went in search of them."

She started to scan the people she could see, looking for the two of them.

"Well, Benson told me they were taking survivors from the same general areas for each room, so they might be here. Although there are hundreds of rooms on this ship alone and I doubt they will let us go wondering from one to another. You want me to help you look in this room?"

"In a minute," she said, working on another cookie. "I think I need to get some more food in me. I was moving bodies out of a lodge near the cave and when I finished I just took a shower and climbed into bed. I flat forgot to eat."

"I never seem to have that issue," he said, laughing. "I love to cook, actually."

"Seriously?" she asked.

She flat couldn't believe this guy sitting in front of her. More than likely he was married or gay or something. That had been her luck with the very few men she had been attracted to.

He nodded. "As we've been traveling, I've collected all kinds of recipes from different worlds. On our ship I have a gourmet kitchen."

She smiled because he seemed to be extremely proud of that fact.

"Family or significant other at home?"

"Mother and father," he said. "No one else."

Again those green eyes of his bored through her and she just couldn't look away.

"So you are an inventor?" she asked, finally letting herself think of something besides how incredible this man was.

"Sort of," he said. "A couple doctorate degrees in mathematics and physics tends to shove a person in that direction."

"I suppose it would," she said.

Now she *really* couldn't believe this guy. Not only was he fantastic looking, but he was as smart as they came.

"We're moving," he said, pointing at the window.

The big room slowly went silent as everyone turned to watch as the planet seemed to suddenly get smaller. Then for a brief instant the stars blurred.

Then without even a sense of movement the stars came back and the planet and sun were completely gone.

Callie just sort of shook her head, not having a clue as to what had just happened.

Around them the room burst into noise.

A few people started crying.

The skinny guy who Fisher had called Doc came running over all excited.

"Did you see that?" he asked Fisher. "No sense of movement, instant trans-tunnel jump. Amazing."

"I saw it," Fisher said. "Can you get *The Lady* to do the same thing?"

"I'm going to stay here until we can," he said, laughing like a little kid.

Then he moved away, going back to talk to some of the crew.

"My friend gets excited easily about space drives," Fisher said, again turning and smiling at her.

"I can see that," she said, smiling. "Where do you think we are now?"

Fisher shrugged. "A safe distance away from that second wave. Maybe a light year or so outside your system."

Callie just looked at him, stunned to her core. He said that so casually.

All in one day she had experienced more death than she wanted to ever see again and taken a ride into deep space on an alien space ship.

And in doing so met a man of her dreams.

When she woke up finally, she was going to have to write all this down.

13

FISHER COULD NOT BELIEVE that he was managing a conversation with this beautiful and very smart woman. More than likely it was because she was in such shock from all the events that she was even paying him the slightest bit of attention.

Yet she seemed interested.

He honestly didn't know when a woman was interested or not in him. He had been blind to relationships for so long, he now found himself completely unprepared when he found someone interesting.

Yet she had been through so much, he couldn't imagine how she was dealing with everything. Her basic core beliefs were no doubt being shattered, not counting the fact that billions of people had died on her planet.

"I think I'm ready to see if I can find my students," she said to Fisher after finishing her sandwich and all but one of the cookies he had brought her. "Would you mind helping me?"

"I would love to," he said, smiling.

He wanted to help her to her feet, but refrained. She seemed to be fine and had power now in her movements and walk.

Side-by-side, they stared around the outside of the room. She gave him a quick description of what they looked like, and it took them almost thirty minutes to wind through the groups of people standing and sitting.

With some survivors, the smell of death was very strong. Other survivors just lay on blankets or sat in chairs with their eyes closed.

When he and Callie had made it three quarters of the way around the big space, it was clear to him that her students were not there.

"Ahh, well," she said. "I hope they are all right."

"I'm sure they are," Fisher said, leading her back over to the two chairs they had left.

They sat and talked for a while about her teaching and where the cave was in comparison to where she taught and so on. He loved to hear her talk and he could tell that the love for her profession was amazing.

"So what were you doing clearing out a lodge by yourself?" he asked.

She took a small bite of the last cookie on her plate. "This lodge and cave is a long ways up in the mountains. My students left, going in search of family. When they called me from about fifty miles away to tell me the death was everywhere and they were continuing on, I knew I was going to have to take care of myself for some time to come. So with no other place to go, I figured the lodge would do fine since it had heat and food to last me for some time."

He nodded. "So you had to clear out bodies to make the lodge livable? How many?"

"Nineteen," she said softly.

"Oh, my, how did you do that?" He couldn't believe she had managed that. He doubted he would have been able to.

She shrugged.

"You don't look big enough to manhandle human bodies."

"A big food cart," she said. "And protective clothing. I did what I had to do. But when I was finished, I locked up the lodge and took a shower and crawled into bed. Completely forgot to eat."

"You think you can survive in that lodge for some time?"

"Maybe a half year or more," she said. "At least through the coming fall and winter."

Then she looked at Fisher and her wonderful brown eyes were wide and she looked like she was about to panic.

"They are going to put us back, aren't they?"

Fisher nodded. He didn't know what else to say.

"And we're not going to remember any of this, are we?"

"They tell me no," he said.

She actually shuddered.

He reached over and put his hand on her hand.

Her skin felt wonderful, but her hand was shaking.

"Tell you what? Let me ask if you can stay with Doc and me. We have a lot of extra room on *The Lady*, entire suites, actually, and maybe we can find a way from up here to help out your planet even more."

"You would do that for me?" she asked.

He squeezed her hand and let go, even though he didn't want to. "Of course."

"Let me go get it cleared so you don't have to worry about it." He stood and smiled at her, the most beautiful woman he had ever met.

"Thank you," she said.

"My pleasure," he said. "I'll be right back."

He was halfway across the room when he noticed the stars outside had blurred and suddenly the planet was back below the ship.

His stomach twisted as he quickly searched for someone who seemed to be in charge, without luck.

Then, as he was about to turn back to Callie, every survivor in the room vanished at once, leaving only the staff.

Across the room Doc shrugged.

Fisher just stood there, staring at the empty chair where Callie had been.

The woman of his dreams was gone.

And now she would never remember him.

Yet he would always remember her.

PART
TWO

14

THE LIGHT STREAMING IN the window woke Callie.

She had had the worst dream, about dead bodies and having to move them and put them in a truck.

She rolled over and yawned and stretched, then opened her eyes.

And instantly she was in full panic mode.

She was in the lodge.

It hadn't been a dream.

She was alone and everyone was dead.

She sat up in the bed and looked at the sweatshirt and sweatpants she had on.

They were a dead woman's clothes.

She lay back, pulled the covers up to her chin, and tried to force herself to just breathe.

"No panic," she said out loud to the large suite.

Her voice echoed and sounded strange to her ears.

"No panic."

Deep breath.

"No panic."

Deep breath.

That helped some.

She opened her eyes and forced herself to look around, focusing on every detail of the room to make herself calm down.

The room had high ceilings, with polished logs as beams. The walls were painted an off white and were decorated in old photos of the early days of the lodge.

There was a living room just off the bedroom to her left with large overstuffed furniture including a couch with soft cloth that looked big enough to sleep two end-to-end.

The floors were old polished wood and had area rugs on both sides of the bed and in the living room under the furniture.

A bathroom with tile floors and old-style sinks was to her right.

The sunlight streaming in the windows meant it was the middle of the day because this time of the year the sun was only over the valley directly for three hours. The rest of the times the tall peaks on three sides of the lodge blocked the sun.

The two main rooms of the suite were lit with wooden chandeliers hanging from wood beams and there were a number of table lamps in various places.

She had left the overhead lights on last night, she remembered that. If she was going to stay here, she was going to need to replace those table lamps with oil lamps pretty soon. Unless she could keep the generator working and there was enough fuel for it.

She climbed out of bed and in her socks went into the bathroom. Then she pulled on some slippers the hotel furnished that were in one closet and went in search of her cell phone.

It was on a wooden table in the main living room area.

No calls, so she tried to call Jim.

His phone rang, and then after a moment he picked up.

"They are dead," he said, his voice soft. "Everyone in the city is dead. My baby is dead."

"I am so sorry," Callie said.

There was a soft sobbing sound on the other end of the call and then the phone went dead.

She looked at the phone, trying to figure out if there was anyone else she could call while the power and cell phones still worked.

There wasn't one damn person outside of Oregon she could think of.

And if Bill had found everyone in Eugene dead as well, then this death had spread far, far wider than she could imagine.

She was alone.

At least for any foreseeable future.

She took her cell phone and went back to the large featherbed. She put the phone on the nightstand and plugged it in, just in case.

Then she crawled back in bed, pulled the covers up over her head, and pretended nothing had happened, letting herself just breathe in the soft smell of lilac fabric softener from the sheets.

She had been strong last night while moving the bodies.

She didn't need to be strong today.

After an hour of feeling sorry for herself and feeling very, very alone, her bladder again forced her into the bathroom. She sure didn't remember drinking that much before going to bed.

But she did need to eat. She hadn't eaten anything before going to bed, but she wasn't hungry. That didn't matter. In this situation, not eating wouldn't help anything.

And she was going to need to do some inventory. She started to run down some chores as she put on her tennis shoes.

She needed to get enough wood in to keep the fireplace going for many long months.

She needed to find oil lamps and as much fuel for them as she could find.

She needed to do an inventory of the food supplies and when all of it was going to spoil.

And she needed to see if she could find a few more clothes and some winter clothing as well.

In other words, she needed to know how long she could hole up here in this lodge before she needed to go down into the valley and then on back to Eugene and the University.

She hoped that she was going to be able to stay long enough for the smells to mostly pass.

She headed out into the hallway toward the big front desk. There would be paper there to do lists. She could use the big wooden front desk as a sort of survival command center.

After all, she was in charge of this place now.

Then, with a notebook in her hand and a pen behind her ear, she headed downstairs to the kitchen and dining areas.

She was going to survive this, whatever had happened. And to do that, she had to take care of herself.

That meant eating regularly.

Even though she just wasn't the slightest bit hungry for some reason.

FISHER COULDN'T BELIEVE what had just happened.

Callie was gone. Sent back into the death below, and he really had no idea where she was. She had described some lodge in the mountains near a cave. But that was all he knew. He didn't even know what part of the planet that lodge and cave were on.

He hoped that the people running the transport beams knew where, but how would he even identify her to them?

He needed to find her, but that was going to take some work and he had a hunch a lot of luck. He was looking for one person among two million survivors on a very large planet.

And he didn't want to think about the problems he would face if he did find her. She wouldn't remember him or anything about this room.

He stared at the chair where she had been. The task of finding her seemed impossible, but those wonderful eyes and the feel of her just wouldn't leave his mind.

He had to try.

He would never forgive himself if he didn't at least try.

He went to a person who seemed to be in charge of the room and asked him what the designation for this room was.

The older bald guy who had on a white smock and who smelled like death just stared at him. The guy seemed far too tired too care about any stupid questions and he looked at Fisher like he had lost his mind.

But then he said, "L-266."

"What department or which person could I talk to about what part of the planet the people in this room came from?"

"Head of transport," the guy said and turned away.

Fisher thanked him as the guy walked toward a door.

Fisher then headed back to where Doc was still talking to a couple of the volunteers.

Fisher had no idea how to move around in this big ship, or if he and Doc were even allowed to. He even had no idea how to get to *The Lady* if he wanted to. They had been transported into this room and hadn't left it yet.

Talk about feeling helpless.

And trapped.

For all he knew, this Benson guy was just going to put them back on their ship, erase their memories as well, and toss them back into orbit.

"That was one of the main people in their engineering department," Doc said, smiling and clearly excited. "Nice guy. He said he would work with me on getting our drives up a notch."

At that point Benson walked into the room, clearly looking tired, but also smiling.

"Rescue a success?" Fisher asked him.

Benson really smiled at that question. "Completely. We managed to rescue over two million people and put them back without losing one person."

Fisher just shook his head. "That's amazing."

"It is, isn't it?" Benson asked. Then he laughed.

"So, let's get you two settled so we all can get some rest."

Benson indicated that they should follow him and he led them out into a corridor outside the room.

There was a wide corridor that seemed to go off into the distance with a number of branching corridors. Fisher had no doubt he could get very, very lost in a ship this size.

Numbers of crew, many in white smocks, were walking slowly along the corridor. And then as Fisher watched, one touched a wall and vanished.

Benson stopped beside a blank panel on the wall. Fisher could see them spaced evenly on both sides of the wide corridor.

"I have given you both special crew status," he said, "so you can stay on board as long as you would like. Talk to anyone you would like, and move freely about. I will be available for questions when you have them."

"Thanks," Doc said, smiling.

"Yes, thank you," Fisher said, not really believing what he was hearing. At least not fully.

Benson pointed at the blank wall screen. "Touch it anywhere."

Fisher reached out and touched the screen. It came to life, showing his name and "Special Crew" status beside his name.

"Some key words the computer is trained for specifically," Benson said. "The main ones are Location, Destination, and Transport. Location tells you where you are at on the ship."

He nodded for Fisher to say that to the screen, so Fisher turned and said, "Location."

A map of the deck appeared on the screen with a designation as to where exactly they were standing. There were letters with three numbers after every location. The room they had just left was L-266 as the man had told him. The panel they stood at was L-267. The next one down the hallway was L-268 and so on.

"We are on L-Deck," Benson said. "There are fifteen major decks. Your ship is on O-Deck. Actually, it is at O-110. So say to the computer the word destination followed by that number. Then say two to accompany you."

Fisher turned slightly again to the board. "Destination O-110. Two to accompany."

The hallway vanished and they were standing beside a bulkhead. "The Lady" sat looking alone and very small on the big landing deck.

"Now that's nifty," Doc said, smiling.

"Would you two like to have rooms on the ship or stay on your own ship?" Benson asked.

"I think we'll be fine on our ship," Fisher said. "We're sort of used to it."

Benson nodded. "I figured as much. Feel free to roam around and talk to as many people as you would like starting in about eight hours. It will take me that long to get some sleep and tell everyone that you two are free to come and go. And the computer board will help you find any department you want to visit."

"Thank you for your kindness," Fisher said.

"Never hurts to have young, fresh ideas around," Benson said. "So we'll be glad to help you if you two can help us in return with anything you see that can be improved on."

"How long are we staying in orbit over this planet?" Fisher asked, suddenly worried that he was going to end up a very long distance from Callie.

"I'm afraid we're going to be here for some time," Benson said. "We are the ship assigned to stay in orbit and monitor the situation. All the other ships will be heading back to their home worlds over the next few days."

"Fine by me," Doc said, nodding.

"Perfect," Fisher said. "And again, thanks."

"Thanks for your help today," he said, and with that he tapped the board, said, "Destination A-19. One to transport."

And he was gone.

Fisher just stared at the spot where he had been standing, then looked at Doc.

"Can you believe any of this?" Doc asked, shaking his head and laughing.

"I'm not sure what to believe anymore," Fisher said as they turned and headed the short distance to their ship.

But all he could really think about was Callie. He hoped she was doing all right.

16

CALLIE SPENT an hour downstairs, forcing herself to munch on an apple and a half sandwich and a fruit drink. While she ate she did a partial inventory, but decided that while it was still light and sunny outside, she needed to go look around the lodge and see what she could see.

Last night, while carrying out the bodies and putting personal effects with them, she had pulled out and kept every key ring from every person. She had a sack of them sitting on the counter in the kitchen, so she took the sack, went back upstairs and got her coat that she hadn't worn while moving bodies, and went outside, making sure to leave the front door of the lodge open so she could get back in without breaking out a window.

The day was beautiful, the sun was bright and still an hour from ducking behind a ridgeline. She didn't need the coat, so she took it off and left it on the porch.

She walked around the lodge as much as she could, considering that it was built hanging out over a ravine, checking it and making a note to get the canned fruit she had unloaded from the truck inside when she had time in the next few days.

Then she started up the road past the front of the lodge toward the parking lot.

There was a long building just up the hill from the lodge that the rangers and some staff lived in. She went up the front steps and pulled open the main door of that building. The smell of death drove her quickly back down the steps and into the fresh mountain air.

Clearly a number of people were dead in there.

She blew her nose and stood and took deep breaths of the fresh mountain air to clear what she could.

That was what the lodge would have smelled like in a very short time if she hadn't worked quickly yesterday to clear it.

She went up into the main parking lot.

There were almost twenty cars there, plus the truck she had parked last night.

She walked a wide circle out and past the truck with all the bodies, then went to the first car, a modern Dodge van. It took her a while to find the right key ring, but she got it open.

Except for a couple of suitcases in the back, there wasn't much. It looked like it was an elderly couple who owned the van, more than likely the two she remembered seeing with the tour group in the opening to the caves. There were a couple of coats she might be able to use, some tools like a shovel and an ax, and some bags of travel snacks between the front seats.

She started to pull them out, then realized that with twenty cars to get supplies from, she might as well use the van to transport it all down to the lodge.

She opened the back gate of the van wide, put the tools on one side, the suitcases on the other, the coats in the back seat, and then moved on to the next car.

The sun was behind the mountain and the air was getting a chill in it before she had gone through every car.

She now had lots of bags of snacks and crackers and different forms of food that would last for a very long time.

She also had half-dozen small shovels and other tools, including a dozen small medical kits.

She had found over twenty winter coats of various sizes and shapes.

And she had the back of the van piled with seven suitcases with women's clothing in them.

She had also found six iPods with a lot of different forms of music already loaded on them and two car chargers that she could use to charge the iPods up when she needed.

When she found the first one she had suddenly realized that the silence around her was weighing on her.

She needed music. She often worked in her office with music going.

She needed to set music up in the lodge, make the place feel more alive.

She liked all sorts of music, so it didn't much matter.

Then it dawned on her that she might want to see if she could get any radio news.

She went back to the van, stared it up and sat, working her way through the dial. There seemed to be two stations still working playing automated play lists. Not one bit of news or emergency broadcast information.

Even though she came up blank, she was annoyed at herself that she hadn't thought of that last night. She clearly was still in shock and not thinking at times. She needed to be very careful.

She was about to close up the van and drive it down to the lodge when she noticed another building with more cars in front of it up the hill to one side of the public parking lot.

More Forest Service buildings, she had a hunch. And maybe employee parking.

She took a Snickers candy bar from one of the snack bags and headed up the hill toward the cars.

About halfway up there, it just seemed to be getting too dark, so she decided she would save those for another sunny day and turned around. She wanted to get the lodge ready for the power to go out.

And she didn't want to do that after dark just in case the power went out tonight.

Ten minutes later she had the van parked outside the kitchen exit and was unloading the supplies of food from the front seat.

Then she headed upstairs to turn on lights and get some music going in the main lobby.

And maybe she would start a fire in the fireplace.

She was going to survive this. She didn't know for what. But survival now was all that mattered.

To do that she had to stay focused.

And be careful.

FISHER'S DREAMS were of Callie. Her smile, her being lost on a planet covered in death.

He woke up with his sheets wrapped around his legs.

He glanced at the clock and realized that he had been asleep for almost nine hours. When they had gotten back in the ship last night, he had taken a shower and then just fell into bed.

Now suddenly, he felt wide awake and not really believing that yesterday had happened. One minute he and Doc were visiting a new planet, the next minute they were helping rescue people and he was falling in love with a woman he lost a few hours later.

He wondered if anyone on the ship had recorded what had happened in the big meeting room with all the survivors. If so, he might be able to get a picture of Callie to hold onto, and maybe with a picture of the two of them together help convince her that he had met here when he found her again.

If he found her.

He was honestly more worried about her not believing him or talking to him than finding her, but even that might turn out to be almost impossible, depending on the records the people on this big ship kept of the transports of the survivors.

He took a shower and then dressed in casual jeans and a short-sleeved blue dress shirt, he headed for the kitchen.

Doc was there, sitting at the big table sipping an orange juice and working on something on a pad.

"Up long?" Fisher asked and Doc shook his head.

"So damned tired, I passed out."

"That makes two of us. Let me fix us some breakfast and we can do some exploring of our host's big ship."

"Sounds perfect," Doc said, his voice clearly excited. "I feel like I got a ton to learn. Like I'm starting school all over again. What about you?"

"I've got a woman to find first," Fisher said.

"The survivor you were sitting with?" Doc asked, for the first time looking up from his pad. He looked almost surprised.

"Yeah, she was amazing," Fisher said, smiling at his best friend, then turning to start some breakfast.

Over the next thirty minutes he fixed a light breakfast of eggs, toast, and some cooked ham for both of them while telling Doc about Callie. It felt great talking about her and by the time he was done, he knew for certain he had to find her and fast. Doc offered to help as much as he could.

Then they headed out of *The Lady*, across the small deck, and to the board on the wall.

"Transportation Department location?" Doc asked.

Fisher smiled. It was nice to have his friend helping him. At least to start. He had no doubt that Doc would get distracted quickly and head off into some sort of space-warp mechanics, but it was great he was willing to help out to start.

The computer showed them the deck and number.

"Security department location," Fisher asked.

The board showed him C-226.

"Wondering if they were recording the room?" Doc asked.

"Exactly," Fisher said. "That way transportation will know exactly where in the room she was."

"Perfect," Doc said. "Let me have a shot at this."

Then Doc turned to the board. "Two to transport to C-226."

A moment later Fisher found himself and Doc looking at a large room of people sitting at what seemed to be large u-shaped consoles. There had to be fifty people in the room, all seemingly focused and busy.

"Wow," Doc said. "That actually worked."

Fisher felt the same way, just staring at the board and then back at the room.

"You must be our new guests on board that Benson informed us about a few hours ago."

The voice came from behind them, so Fisher and Doc both turned to face a man in a blue jacket with some sort of insignia on it. He was smiling and extending his hand.

He couldn't have been more than five foot tall and looked like he had a gut on him that left any room far before he did. He also had white hair that seemed to ring a bald spot like someone had dropped hair removal drops right in the middle of his head.

"I'm Calvin, head of security for 'The R-12."

Fisher introduced himself and Doc and shook the man's hand, then asked, "The R-12?"

Calvin laughed, his stomach shaking. "That's the name of this ship. We built it so fast to get here, no one ever got around to actually naming it and the construction number just stuck. So why the honor of the stop here first this morning?"

"I was wondering," Fisher said, suddenly nervous for some reason, "if you recorded the events in all the survivor rooms yesterday?"

"Sure did," Calvin said.

"Would it be possible to get an image of myself in L-266 talking with a woman survivor there?"

"Sure," Calvin said, smiling as he turned and headed toward a desk. "Thinking of making a rescue of your own?"

"If I can find her again," Fisher said. "And if she'd come with me."

He nodded. "Not going to be easy. But it is possible. I've heard there are about ten people up in transportation working on a similar idea as we speak. Smart to come here first."

"So it wasn't possible for some people to just not be beamed back?" Doc asked, looking at me with a puzzled frown.

"Nope," Calvin said. "Transporting that many people in such a short time had to be done by a computer program. Anyone beamed to the ship had to be sent back down to the exact same position they left from. Their memories were fogged and they were put to sleep. No other way to handle that many people in time to save everyone."

"Makes complete sense," Doc said.

"That it does," Fisher said, feeling relieved that he hadn't failed Callie by not finding someone in time to stop her return.

Calvin was bent over a panel, staring at a screen that Fisher couldn't see.

"What part of the room?"

"Near the window, about in the center."

"There you are," Calvin said.

A moment later Calvin reached under the terminal and pulled up an image of Fisher sitting talking with Callie. It felt like a normal piece of paper, only the image was a top-level photograph.

"I can see why you want to track her down," Calvin said, smiling as he handed Fisher the paper.

"Wow," Doc said.

All Fisher could do was just stare at the image in his hands. It was as if the photo was taken looking over his shoulder directly into Callie's face.

She was looking at him with those fantastic eyes, and she was smiling at him.

"Thank you," Doc said to Calvin.

Fisher managed to pull his gaze away from Callie long enough to say thanks as well.

"Just tell transportation that she was in Sector 3160 of L-266," Calvin said, smiling at Fisher. "And be patient with them. They are jammed."

Fisher again thanked Calvin and then followed Doc over to the panel on the wall.

All he could do was stare at the image in his hands.

"We'll find her," Doc said. "Then it's going to be up to you to convince her to come up here?"

"If I do find her, do we have room on *The Lady*?" Fisher asked. "And will it be all right with you?"

Doc just laughed. "It's about time, don't you think, that we use some of those extra suites we built?"

Then he turned to the board and transported them to the people Fisher hoped would help him find Callie once again.

18

THE ROOM FISHER AND DOC found themselves in was crowd-ed. It was much smaller than the huge security area and had a dozen u-shaped stations with one person behind the station and a second sitting close by looking anxious.

There were four others standing to one side, leaning against the wall.

A woman behind the closest desk looked up and smiled at them. She had bright green eyes and the shortest hair Fisher had seen a woman wear. Being totally bald wasn't far away for her, yet it looked great the way she wore it.

"Looking for someone on the planet?" she asked.

Fisher nodded.

"We'll be with you as quick as we can," she said.

Fisher and Doc stepped over against a wall. Fisher was stunned at how many people were in the same spot he found himself in. And he wondered about all the other ships that were getting ready to leave orbit. What would he be doing if he was on one of those ships right now?

They stood there for a moment before Fisher finally turned to Doc. "No need for you to wait here with me. Head to engineering and I'll meet you back in *The Lady* for lunch in three hours."

"You sure?" Doc asked.

Fisher laughed. "I'm going to be fine. I only talked to the woman for a couple of hours. I might not even like her after I find her again."

Doc laughed. "Yeah, fat chance of that. First woman you've even noticed since you lost all the weight. Trust me, you'll like her."

Fisher glanced at the picture of Callie in his hands and knew his friend was right.

"Lunch," Doc said. He moved over to the big board on the wall and a moment later vanished, off to his real love, engineering.

Four others showed up after Fisher so that the small area around the panel was almost crowded. But people were leaving the desks, some looking sad, others just worried.

Finally a woman wearing a summer-like green dress with short brown hair and sandals came up to the group still waiting and asked, "Who is next?"

It took Fisher a moment and a guy pointing at him before he realized he was next.

He followed her back to her station and she pulled up a chair in front of the monitor and some flat panels. "I'm Raina," she said, giving him a smile that had some of the brightest and whitest teeth Fisher had ever seen. "I assume you are looking to find someone on the planet that you met yesterday?"

Fisher nodded. "L-266, Section 3160."

He handed her the photo as she turned and looked at him with surprise.

"We'll that's going to save some time scanning the room," she said, glancing at the picture and handing it back to him. "Thanks for going to security first. Now let's see if I can track back through the data on the transports to find her."

Her fingers danced over the flat panels and on the screen in front of her an area of the planet below appeared.

With each movement of her fingers the image that Fisher could see on the screen focused in closer.

The image was like looking down at a color photo of the surface.

There were red dots everywhere. Fisher assumed the dots all represented a human. There were a lot of them, scattered, and as the screen moved in closer, there were fewer and fewer red dots.

Finally, Raina stopped and sat back, shaking her head. "That's the best I can do. She's one of those thirty-four people."

She touched her board and then a moment later handed him the image that was on her screen. He could also see data on it as to the location on the planet of the image.

"Sorry I couldn't get it narrowed down any more than that?"

He smiled. "She told me enough about her location that this is more than enough. Thank you."

"Well, that's good," she said.

He stood.

She turned and smiled at him. "Glad to be of help and welcome aboard."

He must have looked shocked and puzzled.

She laughed. "Chairman Benson sent images of you and your friend with his announcement."

"Oh," Fisher said, laughing. "Again, thanks."

He started to turn away, then had a thought and turned back. "How would I find some topographic maps of this area?"

He sort of waved the image she had given him.

Her fingers again danced over the screen and she handed him another image with topographic lines and the dots still showing.

"Thanks," he said, again. "Any chance you might have some information about natural features in this area? She survived in a cave and is staying in a large lodge beside the big natural cave."

This time it took Raina a little longer, her face frowning at times in a focused study, but when she turned to Fisher, she was smiling from ear-to-ear with her teeth almost lighting up the room. "You just made my entire day."

She pointed at the image she was handing Fisher. "Big cave, big lodge, one person way up in the mountains of that area, all alone."

Fisher stood there, staring at the image in his hand of a roof of a large lodge, some big parking lots and other buildings nearby, and an area showing a natural cave.

There was a red dot in the lodge.

"I think we found her," Raina said, smiling.

"I think we did," Fisher said, smiling so hard he thought he was going to hurt himself.

He felt levels of relief he didn't realize he could feel. There was just something about Callie that drove him and now that he knew where she was the feeling of relief almost knocked his knees out from under him.

But then he suddenly realized that there might be rules about having a person from a planet come on board The R-12. Did he need special permission?

He looked at Raina. "Now what do I do?"

"You go talk with her. No rules on bringing anyone back from the surface as long as they want to come. They must be willing and want to come with you."

"Well, she won't remember me, but good to know all I have to do is convince her I'm from outer space."

Raina laughed, again showing all those wonderful white teeth. "Yeah, a challenge, but I'm betting you are up for it."

"And when I'm ready to go to the surface, who do I talk to and how do I get back?"

Again Raina gave him that bright smile. "Me. I'll help you with anything you need. It will be my pleasure."

Then she stood and hugged him and he hugged her back.

"Thank you," he said. "I can't thank you enough."

"Just introduce me to her when she comes on board," Raina said.

"Deal," Fisher said, hugging Raina once more, then turning to go.

"See you soon?" she asked.

"Soon," he said. "Very soon."

19

CALLIE WOKE with oldies rock music playing softly from the main room of her suite. Outside her window the light was coloring the top of the ridgeline that she could see. The day looked like it might be another beautiful one.

She lay there on the wonderfully comfortable featherbed, the quilt pulled up to her chin, just thinking.

Last night she had built a fire in the big stone fireplace in the main lodge front room. Then she had pulled over a couple chairs with stands and a couch and circled the fireplace at a distance where the fire would keep her warm, but not too close to take a chance of anything catching fire. She had put a quilt on each chair and two on the couch and oil lamps on both sides of the big stone mantel, two on the ends of the front desk, and lanterns on all the nearby tables.

Plus she had three flashlights that she had found so far. She needed to go search the glove boxes of the cars for more. She had put one flashlight on the coffee table in front of the couch, another on the front desk, and another in her room near her bed.

The fire turned out wonderfully, warming the big room and giving it a glowing orange look and light smoke smell that she just loved. And between the music and the crackling of the fire, she didn't feel the pressure of the silence and being alone as much.

She had taken an estimate of how much firewood she was going to need to have a fire like that every evening all winter long. She didn't have enough, so the task of finding more went to the top of her list of things to start doing. She hoped the other buildings had wood, and that there was some outside someplace, because the idea of her cutting her own wood didn't appeal in the slightest.

She had also done an inventory of all of her food right after a dinner of turkey sandwich and cherry pie. Eating the way she did, she would easily have enough to make it a full year. In fact, she guessed she had enough to make it almost two years if she had to, considering how many cans of different items were in the storage. Her diet would become very bland, but at least she had enough to make it through the winter and into the spring before thinking about what to do next.

And she had a hunch that the other buildings would have food supplies in them as well. She couldn't go into the dorm for the Forest Service people because of the smell until at least next spring. Today she would look at the other cars and the other buildings higher up the valley.

On the big board behind the main desk in the big room she had written in large letters her list of priorities.

Today she also needed to search for more flashlights and batteries and oil for lamps. She had no idea how long the power would stay on, but she bet it wouldn't be long if no one was maintaining the power grid in this area.

And she had no idea how to even turn on the generators in the basement or how much fuel they had. Finding answers to those questions were on her main list, right near the top as well.

She also needed to do a wash-load or two of clothes. She had found a bunch of women's clothes that would fit her in the cars and in the rooms, but some were dirty, as well as her own clothes from the cave. Today was wash day as well as exploring day.

She glanced at the clock. A little after seven in the morning. Time to get moving. She had a lot to do.

By 7:30 she was finished showering and dressed in jeans, tennis shoes, a wool man's shirt, and a light jacket.

She had also put a pair of gloves in her jacket pocket.

The fire in the fireplace was down to only embers that cracked and the music she had left on in the main lobby had shut itself off.

She turned the music on again and set it to shuffle the selections through pop and country songs.

Anything to keep the silence away.

Then she went down to the old lunch room, put her coat and gloves on the counter, turned on the music she had set up down there as well, and went back into the kitchen to cook herself some breakfast.

She was going to use the food that would spoil first, so this morning it was two eggs over easy cooked in butter, a thin slice of ham, and white toast.

She had a hunch that in six months she would almost kill for this kind of breakfast. But right now she was going to enjoy it.

She sat at the lunch counter, listening to a country western album from Blake Shelton and staring out through the trees as she savored her breakfast. Damn she was going to miss eggs.

And ham. And toast.

She shook that thought away and went back to planning the day.

FISHER WENT BACK to *The Lady* with the maps of where Callie was and the picture of her sitting smiling at him.

He spread the maps and picture out on the kitchen table and then went to working on some lunch. Doc wouldn't be back for at least an hour, but that would give Fisher time to think. And he loved to cook and think at the same time.

He couldn't believe he was even considering going after Callie. More than likely under normal, calm circumstances, they wouldn't even get along. But he doubted that.

Those few hours of talking had been really special for him. And she had seemed very interested in him as well and very happy at the idea that she might be able to stay on board with him.

So even if they didn't end up getting along, he owed her the right to decide to come aboard and out of the death below. She could go back at any time if she wanted. He would not hold her.

But the big problem was that she was isolated and wouldn't remember him at all. The only rule about anyone coming from the surface to the ship is that they must want it.

So he had to somehow come up with a way to introduce himself, let her get to know him a little, and then tell her about a spaceship in orbit that she could go to if she wanted.

Just thinking that made him shake his head and laugh. She would think him a nut case and more than likely just shoot him.

And he wouldn't blame her.

So somehow he was going to need to get to know her and that might take time.

And before he could even try that, he needed a ton more information. The biggest question he had was that if he walked up to her on the planet surface, would she understand a word he said? He was sure that the language systems that made them all seem to be speaking the same language was a shipboard feature. He needed to know if he could even talk with her, considering that they were from planets over sixty light years apart.

He took a pad and started jotting down notes of things he would need to know while he worked on a bacon, lettuce, and tomato salad with a fresh balsamic dressing.

Almost exactly on time Doc walked in followed by a tall, thin woman with thick eyebrows and dark black hair. She was almost as tall as Doc and when she smiled, her mouth seemed to just expand her face out sideways.

She had on jeans, a light blouse with a white vest over it, and a badge that said Engineering on the vest.

"Fisher, this is Kalinda from Engineering," Doc said.

He shook her hand and invited her to lunch. Luckily he had made more than enough. "Hope you are up for a bacon, lettuce and tomato salad."

"I would love that," she said, smiling. "Doc said you usually made enough."

"Always," Fisher said.

She had a great voice and a great smile and she seemed to continually be staring at Doc.

And Doc seemed to be returning the interest just fine.

"Kalinda has been helping me understand some of the basics of their trans-tunnel drive," Doc said.

She just shook her head and laughed. "That took about three minutes, then he started asking questions that a couple of us had never thought to ask. We got permission from Benson to have him work with us."

"It's going to be a blast," Doc said, the smile so large, Fisher thought he might hurt himself.

Doc had always been in his own personal heaven working on higher levels of physics and subspace and warp space technologies. And now it looked like he found a woman that might be able to keep up with him.

"Did you find her?" Doc asked, picking up the map on the table.

"Thanks to a wonderful person by the name of Raina in transportation, I found her."

Both Doc and Kalinda applauded.

"Doc told me what you are thinking of trying to do," Kalinda said, staring at the picture on the table. "She's beautiful."

"But she's not going to remember you," Doc said, sitting at the big table and motioning for Kalinda to do the same.

She went over and sat beside Doc, leaving the chair across from them open.

Fisher doubted Doc noticed, but it was clear that Kalinda wanted her and Doc to be a couple. And as far as Fisher was concerned, that was fantastic.

"Nope, she won't remember me," Fisher said as he served them salads in bowls with the dressing tossed in. "And she has to want to come back to the ship on her own free will. That's the only rule."

"Ouch," Doc said

Kalinda just shook her head. "So you can't just bring her up and then convince her to stay after she sees all this."

"Nope," Fisher said, his stomach twisting so much he wasn't sure he could eat. "I got to let her know I'm a space alien and that she should zip away with me to the stars."

Kalinda laughed softly, but Fisher could see in her eyes that she understood his problem.

"What can we do to help?" Doc asked.

Fisher just shook his head. "Not a thing I can think of. Just keep learning and I'll let you know when I head for the planet and when I get back. Think you can feed yourself while I'm gone?"

Kalinda just patted Doc's hand on the table and he looked at her with a fond smile and a slight puppy-dog stare.

"I'll show him how to use The R-12's mess and boards for snacks," Kalinda said to Fisher. Then she looked into Doc's eyes with a smile. "But trust me, he won't get anything like this wonderful salad."

"Thank you," Fisher said, nodding to Kalinda.

She smiled back and Fisher liked her even more.

And from there they talked about engines and mathematics and everything but the task that faced Fisher.

How was he going to convince a very smart woman who was alone in the mountains after seeing a lot of death that he wasn't from her world, that humans existed beyond her planet, and that she should leave the planet with him.

Yeah, that was going to be easy.

And if he did anything slightly wrong, he would lose any chance of being with Callie forever.

Scared didn't begin to describe how he felt.

AFTER BREAKFAST, Callie headed out to search for firewood and other items on her list.

Near the downstairs kitchen entrance that she had taken the bodies out of was a double door that led into an area of the basement. It took her a while sorting through all the keys before she found the right one and got the door open.

Inside was a room the size of a double car garage and on both sides stacked as high as she could reach was freshly cut firewood, all up off the ground on wooden pallets.

"Score," she said, laughing and clapping her hands together. The lodge had already brought in their wood for the winter, so she was ready to go.

In the back of the garage area was another locked door that didn't take as long to get open because she now had the right key ring, more than likely from the person behind the desk upstairs, or one of the cleaning workers she had moved out.

She opened the door and was stunned. There had to be at least four rifles in there with ammunition under them and two shotguns. There were also knives and other things needed to dress out an animal.

Not once in her life had she fired a gun and didn't much care for them. But standing there, staring at those rifles, she suddenly realized that maybe, just maybe, she should have a way of defending herself.

If not from wild animals, from other humans.

The thought made her shudder, but she still picked up the smallest rifle. The boxes of shells under it said "22 caliber" it, so she took a number of boxes of shells and the gun, locked the closet back up, then locked the wood doors, and went back upstairs.

She stored the rifle under the front desk and put the shells beside it.

At some point in the near future she would practice with it a little bit, see if she could even load it.

But not today.

She went back outside, fired up the van that she had used the day before to transport supplies, and headed up the road toward the big parking lot again. She kept the windows rolled up, but still a couple times along the way she had to cover her nose from the smell coming from the bodies in the forest service building, the two still in the lot, and those down in the entrance to the cave.

She went all the way to the top of the lot to where the other building sat. It looked like it had been a large cabin at one point and had been converted to offices in the front.

She decided to go through the cars first. She found more snacks, mostly bagged chips and candy bars. She also found two flashlights and a couple more coats.

She looked up at the building, almost afraid to go up and try the door, then decided she might as well.

She climbed the ten steps sniffing with each step. So far the air was clear.

She looked through the windows along the porch into the building and could see no one dead in there. Just a few desks and a small kitchen area off to the back.

Finally, taking a deep breath and holding it, she tried to open the front door.

It was locked.

Could she get so lucky as to have no one dead in this building?

She spent a good ten minutes going through keys before she found the right one.

Again taking a deep breath, she opened the door.

No smell. Just a smell of closed up and musty.

So the cars out front were for the workers down in the other building.

She explored the four offices on the main floor, finding two more rifles, a couple flashlights, and some containers of paraffin for the oil lamps that were scattered around the room.

All of the lamps also seemed full, so they would help with light if she couldn't find more fuel down in the lodge.

In the kitchen there were more supplies, but nothing fresh. All canned and packaged food, which she was happy to see.

Upstairs there were two dorm rooms, one had women's clothes in a suitcase. But the woman had been very tall and very large and Callie just left them since she was convinced none of it would fit her at all.

More blankets, more bedding, nothing else.

She took what she needed out to the van, closed and locked the building back up, and then went down to where the cars were parked.

Moving quickly to avoid as much of the smell as she could, she checked the glove boxes for flashlights, finding two more.

By ten in the morning she was back at the lodge and had a load of laundry going in one of the big machines.

As she was taking a long drink of water from a bottle of water, it suddenly dawned on her that she was forgetting a couple of very major areas of survival that she needed to deal with first.

Water and sanitation.

With enough water she could make toilets work. And take baths. But did she have enough water?

And could she get it when the power failed?

The idea of not having enough water suddenly had her feeling very panicked.

She grabbed two candy bars and another bottle of water. Munching on a Snicker's Bar, she went in search of how the lodge supplied its water.

She couldn't believe she hadn't thought of that before now.

What else was she forgetting?

22

FISHER SPENT the next few hours downloading and studying the area around where Callie was held up, including pictures of the lodge.

Then he went back to talk with Raina in transportation. She was very glad to see him and got him back to her station at once.

"You about ready to go?" she asked.

"Getting there," he said.

Today Raina had a maroon scarf around her neck that both accented her short brown hair and her dark dress. And like the first day, she was wearing sandals.

"What I need is information about how the transport to the planet surface is going to work."

She pointed toward the back of the room. "Back there we have a transport room that will transport you to any spot on the planet's surface simply by asking. No waiting."

He nodded.

She held up a small button about the size of the end of his little finger. "We plant this under your skin, normally on the inside of an upper arm where it won't get accidently triggered. You press it in a certain set manner and it will automatically transport you back to the ship and the transport room."

"And if I can get her to agree to come up with me?" Fisher asked.

"You simply say that you have two to transport and hit the button and we bring her along. Just as it is done on the panels around the ship."

"Great," Fisher said.

At that moment he noticed that Raina's eyes got slightly bigger and he turned around in time to see Benson come up behind him.

Fisher and Raina both stood.

"Chairman Benson," Raina said, nodding slightly.

Fisher glanced at her. He had no idea why she called him Chairman. Clearly he had been so focused on getting Callie on board, he hadn't bothered to learn much about this big ship. And suddenly this little voice was warning him that maybe he needed to spend some time and do just that.

"Just wanted to check and see how it's going with your search for the woman you were talking with," Benson said, smiling at Fisher. "Now that I have a little time to breathe again."

"Raina is helping me a great deal," Fisher said. "She found Dr. Callie Sheridan and now I'm just trying to figure out a way to approach Callie on the surface without her chasing me away like I was a nut case."

Benson nodded. "The planets at this level are very suspicious and fearful of possible alien attacks. In a different universe, I suppose it would be justified. Anything I can do to help?"

"Actually," Fisher said, "Raina is doing a great job on this problem. But I was wondering if I could have a little of your time to get a few questions answered in general."

Benson laughed. "I figured you might have a few thousand questions. And your friend Doc has taken to engineering as if he has worked there his entire life. So I have time now. Let's go to my office."

"Wonderful," Fisher said. He turned to Raina. "I'll be back. Thanks again."

"You are more than welcome," Raina said, smiling.

Benson then said, "Two to my office."

A moment later Fisher stood in a huge office with an entire wall that looked like it was open out to space. Below the blue and green and whites of the planet spun by slowly.

"Never get tired of that view," Benson said, indicating a large chair for Fisher to sit in across a wide wood-looking desk.

"Can I ask why she called you Chairman Benson?" Fisher asked as he sat down, turned slightly so he wasn't distracted from the view.

Benson nodded. "In the Alliance we formed in our sector, we don't have a military structure. We run every ship as a corporation, a business venture. So what would be the Captain is the Chairman."

"Since you plan on being here for a year, how many people live on board?"

"Just under two thousand," Benson said and Fisher was stunned. "A lot of families and we are doing a lot of research and just getting used to this big new ship over the year."

"Wow," Fisher said.

Benson shrugged. "Space has no limits and power is unlimited as well. We are only limited by our imaginations. Which brings me to your partner, Doc. He's amazing."

Fisher laughed. "In more ways than one."

"Just from questions he's asking in engineering, he might help all of us advance in speeds of our ships. Glad you both are interested in staying on board for a while."

"Thanks for having us," Fisher said.

He went on to ask a dozen more questions about the ship, including the one about how everyone spoke the same language.

"Transport," Benson said. "The language is just given to the person being transported."

"That's why we could understand you and think we were speaking our own language?"

Benson nodded. "Exactly. Since all humans on all planets seem to have a basic pattern that their civilizations develop, the language aspect became pretty simple."

Something about all civilizations developing along similar paths bothered Fisher, but he couldn't put his finger on what. So he asked the next logical question he had.

"Has anyone ever gone looking for the Seeders?"

Benson laughed. "Just about every day from every planet out there that has figured out space travel and found out what happened in this galaxy."

"And no trace?"

"Not one item left behind by the Seeders. Nothing. They seeded the galaxy with humans and plants and animal life that took over on each Earth-like planet in the Goldilocks zone of each sun and then seemingly vanished."

Benson tapped what to Fisher looked like a form of computer panel on his desk, then scribbled something on a note pad that everyone on the ship seemed to have and leave around like paper.

Benson then handed the pad to Fisher.

"Doctor Jenny Sins, the top scientist in the department focused on the Seeders search. Go talk with her. Tell her I sent you."

"You have an entire department on the ship for this?"

"Every ship does," Benson said. "The question you asked is that important to all of us. We all know how the universe started. That's just science. None of us have a clue how we got here.

Or for that matter, why?"

FISHER WAS STUNNED when he entered the Seeder Research area of Benson's big ship. There had to be fifty people working in the large room at different stations. He had no idea what they might be doing.

An elderly man with white hair and a formally white lab coat that seemed smeared with some sort of strawberry jam sat at the first desk closest to the entrance. He glanced up and then smiled with a perfect set of teeth. The smile made his face turn into a mass of loose flesh and wrinkles. "You're one of the explorers from this sector, aren't you?"

"I am. Doctor Vardis Fisher," Fisher said, extending his hand. "But everyone just calls me Fisher."

The older man took his hand and shook it, but before he could say anything a woman's voice behind Fisher said, "Well, Doctor Fisher, The Chairman warned me you would be coming."

Fisher turned around to face one of the most beautiful women he could have ever imagined wearing a white lab coat. And over the years he had imagined some pretty amazing women in white lab coats. Never met one, but imagined many.

She looked more like a model that should be posing half-nude in magazines.

"I'm Doctor Jenny Sins," she said, extending her hand and smiling. The smile reached her blue eyes and made her seem radiant. She had long brown hair pulled back into a ponytail, and seemed to be about Fisher's height.

And she was Fisher's age as far as he could tell.

He took her hand and as he said he was pleased to meet her he noticed her wedding ring.

She held his hand for a few seconds too long while she stared into his eyes, then nodded and let go and turned away. "Let me show you what we do here."

Fisher had no idea what that was about.

He followed her and her flowing brown hair and white lab coat as she introduced him to three others in the lab. All seemed very happy to meet him for some reason.

Finally they ended up in a large open office built into one wall of the large room. It was clearly her office and from it she could pretty much see the entire room.

She went around and sat behind a large desk that seemed to have grown out of the floor. She indicated Fisher should take the chair across the desk from her, which he gladly did.

"Well, Doctor Fisher, ask me anything and I'll see what I can tell you."

"It's just Fisher."

She smiled again. "Jenny."

He took a second, then decided which question he wanted to ask first.

"So is it clear where the Seeders started and where they stopped in the Galaxy?"

She nodded and with a few quick taps on a control panel on her desk, an image of the Milky Way Galaxy appeared on the wall to the right.

"They started in this area," she said, and on the map an arrow appeared pointing at some stars on the outer edge of one of the spiral arms of the galaxy.

"They went around the galaxy clockwise, working inward and then outward, and ended in this area."

Again on the image of the galaxy another arrow appeared near the edge of the galaxy.

It was amazing and almost more than his mind could handle. She was talking about an entire galaxy like it was a neighborhood. Billions of stars and more distance than he could almost imagine.

He forced himself to not think of the size they were dealing with and pull his mind back and pretend the galaxy was actually only like a round city.

"Looks like they came into the galaxy," Fisher said, continuing to stare at the image, "did their work, and then left."

She nodded. "Sure seems that way."

"How far into the core of the galaxy did they push?"

"Only as far in as human populations could stand the radiation levels," she said. "But very few of those civilizations in close have survived for very long. Just too much going on in closer to the galaxy core that causes planet-wide destruction."

"Like what we saw below," he said.

"At a vastly more frequent and violent scale," she said, nodding. "The closer to the core of this galaxy, the nastier it gets for human life. They stayed pretty much in the zone conducive for human growth over long periods of time."

"So where do you think they went?"

"Andromeda Galaxy and all the smaller galaxy clusters around it," she said without hesitation.

The map of the galaxy shrunk down to the size of a small dinner plate on the wall allowing the closest neighboring galaxies to be shown. "Looks like they came in from the Large Magellanec Cloud and then headed to Andromeda and all of its satellite galaxies."

He had to admit that it looked that way. Like following a map on a bunch of country roads.

"Anyone go after them?"

"Not that I know of," she said. "Our ships don't have the speed to cross that much distance in a time that would allow us to catch them, even if we were sure where they were headed."

"So how did they do all this?" Fisher asked, trying his best to keep his mind clear and the scale of what he was thinking about under control. "Are we all genetically the same? Everyone on every planet?"

"We all started from the same basic gene pool," she said, again nodding. "And no degradation over time. Every planet's human and animal population started with the same genes, the same diversity, the same numbers. One hundred and forty-four thousand."

There was that number again. He just couldn't seem to make any logical sense out of any of this. There was something very clear he was missing. He knew that feeling. He just had to find what was between the obvious.

"Did they grow our ancestors or something?"

She shrugged. "Lots of theories on that. But what we do know is that it took them six major visits to each planet to accomplish what they did."

"Six?"

She nodded. "On the first visit they shoved some asteroid or something large into every planet that caused a vast extinction event of most of the animal and plant life that was natural to the planet."

"You're kidding?"

She shook her head no. "On the next four visits they covered each planet with new plants at first and then stages of animal life that quickly took over, including early primates."

"How long between that last animal seeding and the introduction of humans?"

"About three thousand years," she said, not even breaking into a smile.

Fisher shook his head. "That is so against all science I know that it's scary."

She nodded. "We are convinced they also seeded historical evidence on every planet of both human, plant, and animal history."

Fisher started to open his mouth to object, then realized where he was sitting and that he was talking to a beautiful human scientist on a huge spaceship light years from his home and even farther from her home.

Historical evidence could be planted. Sitting here was very real and hard to discount.

But wow, planting historical evidence was sure going to make Callie's work as a paleontologist seem almost impossible. Unless maybe she could help find some clues in the planted evidence. She might be able to help him on all this if he convinced her to come on board.

Fisher closed his mouth and just sat there.

"Hard to get a grasp on it all, isn't it?"

Fisher laughed. "I imagine you grew up with this knowledge. I've just been coming to grips with it over the last two years that we have been out here in space exploring."

"That would be difficult," she said, a look of worry suddenly in her blue eyes.

"I'm sure I'll come to terms with it," Fisher said, even though he wasn't so sure. "So how long do you think the Seeders were in this galaxy?"

"Only about fifty thousand years," she said.

That number made no sense to Fisher. "How many planets did they do this to?"

She shrugged. "No firm count. Maybe upward of a hundred million in this galaxy. Maybe ten times that number. No one really knows."

"In fifty thousand years? Holy smokes, how many Seeders were there?"

She shrugged once again. "No one knows that either, but they just finished about five thousand years ago as far as we can tell."

That stunned him even more.

"How long have the races in your sector been in space?"

"About two thousand years," she said. "We just missed them."

"And they didn't leave a trace?" he asked, stunned at what she had told him.

"Just us," she said. "Just us."

24

CALLIE FOUND the water supply for the lodge in about thirty minutes. As she feared, it was an electric pump that seemed to draw water up from a well.

The entire well was tucked in a large room in the basement and off the side that seemed to almost hang over the ravine. She studied the pump for a moment, noticing that it looked fairly new.

Also, on one side of the pump was a small generator.

She opened the fuel cap on the generator and as far as she could tell, the tank was full.

That was good because so far she hadn't found any extra fuel to run any of the generators in the lodge.

It would have been logical that they would have set up this generator to run only when water was required and the power was off. Otherwise, she was going to have to be down here turning it off and on regularly.

From the big well pump, she followed a white-wrapped pipe through a wall and into a large room next door. There was another smaller pump there and the pipe went straight up.

She tried to mentally mark her position in the building and then went upstairs.

The pipe was exposed in a back service area coming from the floor and going through the ceiling to the next floor above.

So she went upstairs.

The pipe again came from below and went directly up through the ceiling.

The pipe didn't seem to be like any vent, but if it wasn't, that meant there was another floor up there under the eves of the lodge.

It took her almost a half hour of searching and opening doors before she found the service staircase.

She followed it up, a flashlight in one hand just in case the power chose this moment to finally go out.

She could stand up under the peak of the roof and there was a wide walkway there. She followed it back to the center of the hotel and there she saw something she couldn't believe.

A large tank. Maybe ten steps across and almost as tall as she was.

The white pipe she had followed up from the basement came up the side of the tank and curved and went into the tank.

There were a couple of metal stairs on one side and she climbed them and opened a metal hatch she found at the top.

Water.

A full tank of water.

All gravity fed. All she had to do was run the generator for the pump to refill the tank at times. And the tank was large enough that it would last her for a very long time.

Her decision to stay in the lodge had clearly been a correct one.

So she closed up the tank and headed back downstairs. Then for the next hour she checked every faucet in every room in the building, making sure nothing was on or even dripping.

Now she needed to find more fuel for the generators. The small one running the water pump had gas in it, so she knew with all the cars in the parking lot, she could refill that one.

But the two larger generators she suspected didn't run on gas. More than likely diesel.

She went back into the basement and checked both fuel tanks on both generators. She was right, both ran diesel and both were thankfully full. Clearly the lodge had been getting ready for the coming winter.

She went back outside. It was just noon and the sun was now hitting the top of the lodge and the valley floor. It was a beautiful day once again.

She started slowly around the lodge, looking for any sign of an underground fuel tank.

Nothing.

She went from the service entrance all the way around past the front door and to the uphill side and out onto a balcony built there off the main lobby.

Cave Creek ran below the lodge, but there wasn't even a trail down the ravine that she could see. All the guests normally went up the hill to the caves. Not down into the ravine.

She went back to the kitchen, made herself a quick turkey sandwich and then, eating it and carrying an apple in her pocket, she headed back out and up the hill, looking alongside the road for any sign of a fuel tank.

There was nothing around the Forest Service dorm building with the bodies in it, so she climbed up through the parking lot and walked around the building above the top of the parking lot.

Nothing there as well.

So the only fuel she had for the two big electrical generators were in them.

She would have to make that last. And charge her electrical devices in the cars.

It wasn't going to be the best, but she could make it work through the winter.

And then next spring she would deal with that future when it got here.

FISHER WENT BACK to *The Lady* and just sat in the kitchen area, munching on the remains of the salad from lunch and trying to figure out what was the best way to approach Callie.

After talking with Benson and then Jenny in the Seeder Research, he was even more convinced he was just flat missing something that was obvious and right in front of him. He hated that feeling. And he had a hunch that from what he understood of Callie's mind and specialty, the two of them might be able to solve what he was missing.

He just didn't know how he was going to convince her to come back here with him.

Finally he hit on an idea.

He spent the next hour studying the area around the lodge, the towns below it, the road in, and the distances involved. And he memorized all the names as best he could.

Then he made sure that his jeans and shirts would match the look of the area and that he had a few days of clothes with him.

He packed that in a backpack, contacted Doc that he was leaving, and with the picture of Callie smiling at him in his pack, he headed for the transportation department. His stomach was twisting in fear, but unless he tried this now, he never would.

And he didn't want to lose the chance of getting to know Callie more. And if nothing else, rescuing her from a very tough number of years on the planet's surface.

Raina greeted him with a smile as he appeared in the transportation department.

"Ready to give it a try?"

"I am. But a couple of questions to make sure my plan will work. If I come back, how quickly can I return?"

"It would take us about thirty seconds to send you back to the exact spot," she said.

Then she smiled. "Vanishing in front of her might well help her decide."

"Or scare her to death."

"Yeah, it most certainly will do that," Raina asked.

"One more favor? Do you have access to the security images of that day when she was on board?"

"Sure," Raina said, sitting back down at her station. "What room again?"

"L-266, area 3160."

Her fingers flew over her board and the same image Fisher had of Callie in his pack came up on her screen.

"Is there a camera showing us both talking with the planet in the background?"

"Again good thinking," Raina said.

On the screen an image appeared a little farther away from the two of them. They were talking and both of them were very clear. Beyond them, out the window, a clear image of the planet.

"Perfect," Fisher said.

She printed it out and he folded it and put it in his pack with the other one.

Then she took him back to the transportation room. It was a giant area with a hundred small platforms lined along both walls separated by narrow partitions.

"Where do you want the return chip?" she asked. "And how many times do you want to hit it as a return call."

"Two clear pushes," he said. Then he raised his arm and showed her where he wanted it to be. Under his arm on his left side, so that his right hand could reach over like he was grabbing his arm and his thumb could push the return key.

She nodded and then before he could worry about something being inserted under his skin, it was already there.

He stared at the slight lump under his skin and felt it, amazed.

Raina smiled. "We can transport full humans and anything we want just about anywhere. Easy to put something just under your skin."

He shook his head. Of course it would be.

"Ready?" she asked.

He nodded.

She had him step up on a nearby platform and as he did a control panel slid up out of the floor in front of the platform and Raina stepped to it.

"Where exactly?" she asked.

"It's midday in the area she's at, correct?" He had checked that a few times, but he wanted to be very sure he didn't arrive in the middle of the night.

"It is," Raina said.

"How about a short distance down the road below the lodge?"

"Perfect," Raina said. "I show her in the lodge right now. Good luck. And remember, two pushes on the return and you come right back here to this platform."

"And no problem going back and forth?" he asked.

"None," she said, smiling.

"Then let's do this before I chicken out."

Raina nodded and her fingers danced on the board and the next moment Fisher found himself standing in fresh mountain air on a narrow paved road.

"Oh, man, now what have I done?" he said out loud as he looked around at the tall pine trees and mountains that towered over the narrow valley.

No one answered.

26

IT WAS JUST AFTER ONE in the afternoon and Callie had just finished making a salad from the last of the lettuce in the fridge when she heard the call. She had added in part of a tomato and hard-boiled an egg and crumbled it over the salad. She had a choice of dressing that had been made up and in the fridge for a few days, but she didn't trust them and used the oil and vinegar instead.

She had just tossed the entire thing realizing she had made far too much for one person when she heard someone shouting. At first she didn't recognize the sound, but then a second "Hello!" echoed through the air outside the lodge.

All she could think about was rescue was here.

Could that be possible?

She left the salad sitting on the counter and scrambled up the stairs and to the main door of the lodge that led out onto the big road.

"Anyone home?"

Another shout echoed through the canyon as she opened the big wooden front door and went out onto the porch.

A lone man stood there in the middle of the road about thirty paces from her, a pack on his back and a smile on his face. He wore jeans, a dark shirt, and what looked like tennis shoes.

He wasn't any sort of rescue, that was for sure. But he was another survivor.

She felt her knees get weak as she smiled back at him.

He was one of the best-looking men she had ever seen. His short brown hair and wide shoulders just made him look sexy standing there in the sun holding the pack on his shoulder. And the smile on his face didn't hurt the look either.

He could have been a model in *GQ Magazine*. Wow!

"Hi," he said, waving, but not coming any closer, which she respected. "My name's Fisher."

His voice was low and sexy as well.

And there was something about that name and his looks that dinged the back of her brain. She felt like she knew this guy from somewhere. She couldn't place where, but she was sure she had seen him or met him before.

Completely sure of it.

"Callie," she said.

"I was hoping others would be alive up here," Fisher said. "I figured the cave might have saved a few."

"It did," Callie said, not telling him that she was the only one here. "Where are you from?"

"Eugene, actually," Fisher said. "I was at the coast when all this happened, so decided to come up here to hole up for the winter. That is if you and the other survivors don't mind more company. If you do, I can go back to the coast."

"Not at all," she said, her heart leaping at the idea she might have company all winter long. "More the merrier."

He stood there, not coming toward her, just staring at her.

And she just kept staring back as the silence of the hills and the warm afternoon closed in around them.

Finally she realized it would be up to her to welcome him. He was being very courteous and not trying to just come up.

Wow, the guy was smart.

And her little voice told her that there wasn't a threatening thing about him.

Sexy yes, but not threatening.

And over the years she had come to trust that little voice when it came to creepy men.

He was far from creepy.

"You hungry?" she asked, breaking the silence of the mountains. "I just made a salad and I got enough for two."

He smiled, looking relieved, and nodded. "I am, actually. Thanks."

"Come on in."

She stood to one side and held the door.

She couldn't believe she was trusting this stranger this much. But he seemed so familiar and nothing about him felt threatening at all. More than likely she had seen him in Eugene around the university.

As he got closer she could see his wonderful green eyes and the smile never seemed to leave his face.

Then suddenly he looked embarrassed and looked down and went past her into the lodge.

As he went inside he said, "Wow, this place is really something."

He stood there, just inside the door, sort of looking around at the high ceilings and massive stone fireplace and log construction.

"It is, isn't it?"

She pulled the front door closed and then indicated that he should follow her down the wooden stairs.

When he saw the old fashioned café with the nifty old counters and the view of the ravine, he again shook his head. "Amazing, just amazing. And the electrical is still on."

"I'm betting not for long," Callie said, leading the way into the kitchen. "You're going to have to tell me what it's like out there beyond this hill."

"Not pretty," he said.

He didn't elaborate, so she grabbed an extra bowl from the cabinet and again tossed the salad, then filled both bowls, still having some left over.

"Last of the lettuce," she said, handing him a bowl and leading him back out into the lunch counter area. "Mixed with a tomato and egg."

"Perfect," he said. "Thanks."

All she could think was that it wasn't the salad that was perfect. He was, and maybe she was dreaming all this out of fear of spending the entire winter alone up here on the side of a mountain surrounded by nothing but trees and death.

He put his pack on the top of the counter and they sat at a table in front of one window.

They ate and talked some, both clearly being careful. She just staring at his strong hands and then up into his green eyes.

Finally she said, "Do I know you from somewhere?"

"It does feel like we have met before," he said, nodding.

And then he smiled and she just laughed.

"I'll remember where," she said.

"I hope so," he said, staring down into his salad.

27

FISHER COULDN'T BELIEVE IT when Callie came running out of the front of the lodge when he shouted. At first he didn't think she was going to answer him.

But then when she came out of the lodge without a gun, he both breathed a sign of relief and was stunned at her beauty once again. Her short brown hair and dark eyes just seemed to draw him in and he had a rough time keeping his voice level.

She was dressed in jeans, tennis shoes, and a heavy blue work shirt that almost looked like it had been a man's shirt with the sleeves rolled up. Last time he had seen her she had been in sweat pants and a sweatshirt and socks. She looked good like this and in the sweats. He had a hunch she would look wonderful wearing anything.

And now, standing in the middle of a road on a different planet, he remembered completely why he was risking so much to try to rescue her.

He was drawn to her more than he had ever been drawn to another person in his life.

He gave her his cover story about being over on the coast, but thinking this might be a good place to find survivors. He felt odd having to lie to her, but at this point he had no choice.

Finally she had invited him in for some lunch and had served him a salad.

Over lunch he managed to get her talking about how she survived in the cave. She had told him the story before, so he was careful to not say anything to get ahead of her.

"You want to see the entire place?" she said after lunch and he had offered to wash the dishes, which she let him do while he asked her questions about her job.

He just liked listening to her talk and it seemed she was very happy for company.

"I'd love to," he said. "How's the water situation?"

"Big tank up under the eaves," she said, smiling like she was happy she had the answer. "Pump from a well on this level with a small generator on it keeps the tank full."

She pointed back behind the kitchen to where the pump room must be.

"So that's good," he said. "How about food supplies?"

"More than enough for the winter," she said.

She led him back upstairs. "I haven't found any reserves of oil or paraffin for the lamps yet, but all of them are full."

She pointed to the lamps she had placed around the lodge and on the front desk.

"Lots of wood?" he asked.

"Again more than enough to make it through the winter."

He nodded.

She stood, staring at him for a long moment. "Where did you teach? You look so familiar?"

"Eugene," he said, sticking with his cover story. "Math department." She nodded, then indicated he should take a seat on one of the couches. "I got some questions I need to ask you."

"Sure," he said, dropping his pack on the couch and sitting beside it. There were two big couches there, all with blankets over the back, and four large, overstuffed chairs. All were grouped around the big stone fireplace and a large wooden coffee table clearly made out of cut pine.

As he sat down, Fisher could feel something had shifted and darned if he knew what or why or what had gone wrong.

She moved around the counter, then quickly pulled out a rifle from behind the counter and aimed it at him.

His stomach twisted into a knot. Somehow he had screwed up and screwed up big time.

"Okay," she said, staying behind the front desk and keeping the weapon leveled at him. "Now for some truth from you before my friends get back."

"Didn't buy my cover story, huh?" he asked, shaking his head and smiling. His best bet was to just remain calm. He doubted she would shoot him, but anything was possible. She was a very strong woman and he had no doubt she would do what she had to do to survive. Including killing him.

"Not in the slightest," she said. "Or at least not for very long. And I know everyone in the Oregon math department. So how about some truth and where do I know you from?"

"Truth?" he asked, deciding to take a chance. "Like you have no friends coming back?"

"Truth," she said, nodding, the rifle in her hands waving.

"You are not going to believe me."

"Try me," she said.

"We met just a day or so ago," he said, doing his best to keep his voice calm. "You were wearing sweat pants and a green sweatshirt and socks. It was the first night when you came out of the caves and had finished clearing the bodies away from inside the lodge."

"I..." she started to say something, but he stopped her. He could tell his statement shocked her, and it hadn't been the best way to start into the truth. But he had to keep going now.

"I know you don't remember that. None of the survivors do. But you were wearing those clothes that night, correct, as you slept?"

She just stared at him.

"I said you wouldn't believe me."

"All right," she said after a moment. "Start at the beginning. What happened to cause all the deaths?"

He sighed. He hated to think about all the death that covered this planet right now. "A star about twenty light years from here exploded, sending out an intense electromagnetic pulse that hit this planet directly and short-circuited human and some animal brains, killing everyone who was out in the open instantly. Only those underground, in ships, bank vaults and places like that survived. There were just under two million survivors of the first pulse."

"First pulse?" she asked, looking very puzzled, but seeming to follow.

"There was a second pulse," he said, glad she was staying with him through this, "so other human planets mounted a rescue operation and got all two million survivors of the first pulse out of the way on ships until after the second pulse went past."

She started to interrupt him, but he kept talking. "Then they erased everyone's memory of the event and put every person back where they were a few hours before. Asleep. You and I spent a number of hours together talking during that rescue operation."

She opened her mouth, then closed it.

"I knew you wouldn't believe me, so I brought pictures, if I may?"

He pointed to the pack, hoping she would let him get out the pictures and not just decide to start shooting.

She nodded and he took out the two pictures and then carefully stood with his hands in the air and put them on the end of the counter away from her, then went back to the couch.

She stared at them, shaking her head.

He had no idea how she would feel about those pictures, but he knew without a doubt they were his best shot at convincing her.

Finally, after what seemed an eternity, she looked up at him with those wonderful brown eyes.

"Who exactly are you?"

At least she wasn't chasing him down the road yet with the weapon.

"My name is Vardis Fisher, but everyone calls me Fisher. I am a mathematician and inventor."

"And where are you from?" she asked. "And is this your natural form?"

He laughed, because he had wondered the same thing when he first met Benson.

"I am from a planet about sixty light years from here. And yes, this is my natural form. My friend and I were exploring when we stumbled onto this rescue operation. We offered to help, but we didn't do much. Except that I talked to you. And I caught you when you turned around too fast and fainted from not eating. And I got you some food."

She again looked blank, but he could tell his truth was getting through a little.

So he went on. "The people up there who are in charge of the big ship I am visiting tell me there are no alien life forms above low-level animal life anywhere in the galaxy. Humans with the same exact genetic make-up as you and I have settled the entire galaxy."

She looked at him for a moment, shaking her head, then back at the pictures, the rifle on the counter in front of her seemingly forgotten, even though it was still mostly aimed at him.

"What reason would you tell me this story?" she finally asked.

"Because you asked for the truth," he said. "Remember?"

"So, if you are telling me the truth, why are you here?"

"Because," he said, "when we were talking, we got along very well. And you said you wanted to stay on board the ship instead of coming back here. I went to get permission from those in charge of the big rescue ship to have you stay, but you were transported back and your memory erased before I could."

"So why don't you just transport me back up to the ship?" she asked, again the gun in her hands.

"Can't," he said. "Anyone coming on board must want to come on board. So I'm here to try to convince you to at least come and take a look. No strings attached."

"And you would erase my memory again when you sent me back here?"

"Nope," he said, shaking his head. "You would be free to stay on the ship or come and go as you wanted."

"And what's in this for you?" she asked.

"Honest answer?" he asked. He was deathly afraid she would get to this question and he wasn't sure how he would answer it.

"After all this, I can't imagine you saying anything that might shock me more."

He took a deep breath and decided on just flat continuing to tell her the truth.

"I was very attracted to you, but we only had a few hours to talk. I would like to have longer to get to know you. And with your brain, I think you would do your planet a better service from space than trapped here in this lodge."

With that she opened her mouth, then just closed it again.

"Second, I have a problem I'm sort of just starting to study about humans settling the entire galaxy. I could use someone with your knowledge and skills to help me figure it out. So that's two reasons. One personal, one professional. But honestly, the personal reason is my number one reason."

He held her gaze and she held his.

Finally she slid the gun a few feet away from her down the counter and he let himself take a slight breath of relief. He had never had a gun pointed at him in his entire life and he didn't much like it at all.

"Can you jump back to this mythological ship at any point, or do you need to wait for a shuttle or something?"

"I can go and come as I want," he said, again holding her gaze.

"Then go back to your ship and give me time to think about all this. Come back tomorrow."

He wanted to jump up and down for joy, but he maintained his composure.

"Can I bring you breakfast and meet you in the kitchen in the morning?" he asked, hoping that she would say yes. It would be more than he could have hoped.

"Why not? Eight a.m."

Again he almost jumped to his feet and shouted "Yes!" But he refrained.

"White or wheat toast?"

She laughed, shaking her head. "White."

"Orange juice?"

"Sure, why not?"

"See you downstairs in the kitchen at eight your time."

With that Fisher touched his return point in his arm twice and the lodge and Callie vanished and the next moment he found himself standing on a platform in the transport center.

Raina ran over to meet him.

"How'd it go?"

"She saw right through my cover story in a flash," he said.

She laughed. "Smart woman."

Then Fisher smiled at Raina, his grin almost hurting his face. "But I'm taking her breakfast tomorrow morning."

28

CALLIE STARED AT THE SPOT on the couch where the handsome and very weird stranger named Fisher had been. He had simply vanished, leaving the pictures and his pack behind.

"Holy crap, Callie," she said out loud, her voice echoing through the lodge. "You're going crazy."

She didn't let herself look again at the two pictures of herself sitting on some sort of spaceship and went around to the couch to look through his pack. There was nothing in there that would confirm that he was either a nut case or a space alien. Just clothes. Two changes of clothes, actually.

And nothing that would tell her that he had the slightest worry about survival. He was clearly someone who had only expected to stay for a day or so, not survive an entire winter.

"Think!" she said. "Think! This can't be real."

She left the pack on the couch and headed out the front door.

The afternoon had turned warm and the sun hadn't yet dropped behind the ridgeline. The warm smell of pine was something she loved as a child and it comforted her now.

She turned and headed up the road toward the parking lot, her footsteps echoing in the silence of the mountains. About halfway to the parking lot the smell of death stopped her cold. She didn't want to see the two bodies in the parking lot and what the heat and animals would be doing to them.

That was real.

The death here that had happened suddenly was very, very real. Not a one of those bodies she had moved the first day out of the lodge had a mark on them.

Something like an electromagnetic pulse had killed them, of that she had no doubt. So his story fit on that one detail.

And somehow he had pictures of her in that dead girl's sweatpants and sweatshirt sitting in a lounge with an image of the planet behind her.

How could he do that?

And why? And how could he be so damn good looking?

She was going crazy.

She turned around, walking fast down the road, away from the lodge and the death.

Finally, a quarter mile down the road she saw a small sports car in the ditch to the inside of the road. A couple was in it, dead, slumped over, their seat belts holding them upward. They looked young. Not as young as the couple she had taken from the bed.

But young.

They had clearly died instantly and their car had just run off the road.

She remembered the call from Jim, how he was sobbing that his wife and kid were dead in Eugene.

She sat down in the middle of the road and just stared at the car and the two bodies inside.

This was very real.

All of it.

The death, the smell, the fact that she was alone.

She hated being out of control and yet now she felt completely out of control.

Her world had ended.

The world she trusted, had depended on, had worked inside.

It was all dead around her.

And now some total stranger claiming to be from space had offered her a way out.

But how could she believe him?

How could she trust him?

She couldn't.

She knew that. She hadn't been good at trusting anyone back when the world was normal. She sure couldn't do it now.

But he had said he was there, sitting in the lodge, talking to her, trying to convince her to go with him.

He said he was attracted to her.

He said he also needed her help professionally on a project.

And he had simply transported away, so clearly he had the technology to transport her as well if he wanted.

But he said she had the choice.

What choice?

She stared at the two bodies in the car. Except for survival, at this point she wasn't sure she had any choice.

But she was going to need more information before she would agree to be spirited away by anyone.

Especially some alien.

Even if he was the most handsome man she could remember seeing.

And unlike the two bodies in the car in front of her, he seemed to be very much alive.

FISHER KNEW THAT the next eighteen hours were going to be eighteen of the longest hours he had ever spent. He hated waiting. So he went to find Doc in engineering.

Both Doc and Kalinda came rushing over to ask how it went and why he was back so quickly. So he told them, then he listened to what they were working on.

From what Fisher could tell, Doc had an idea of putting one trans-tunnel inside another to speed up all flight, and he had everyone buzzing with the idea.

"If this works, *The Lady* will be the fastest ship in this sector," Doc had said at one point.

"Can you get it to stop coming out of a trans-tunnel flight?" Fisher asked, remembering their scary entrance into this system.

"That's easy," Doc said, shaking my head. "Amazed I didn't see how to do that myself."

Kalinda smiled her full-face smile at Doc. "You would have."

Fisher had no doubt that those two were a couple for some time to come. Doc might not know it yet, but Kalinda knew what she was doing and would make it happen. And that made Fisher happy for his friend.

So after killing a half hour with them, he decided to visit Jenny in the Seeder department and let Doc and Kalinda get back to their work.

Jenny managed to get him a number of papers on theories as to why no evidence of the Seeders had ever been found.

And Fisher took two of the top authorities on the theories of how the plants and animals were seeded, as well as how historical evidence was also planted to let cultures think they had been there a very long time. He figured Callie would really be interested in that, once she got over the entire idea of Seeders. And spaceflight. And humans on every planet.

She had a way to go to get through an entire forest of shocking facts. Fisher just hoped he could help her some. And not drive her away by simply telling her some of the stuff.

By the time he got back to *The Lady*, he had used two hours of the eighteen hours.

Somehow he had to keep himself distracted to keep going through the rest of the day and eventually get some sleep before going back to the surface.

So with one of the papers on Seeder evidence playing in his ear, he went to the gym on *The Lady* and worked out for almost two solid hours.

Then after a shower, he cooked Doc and Kalinda and himself a dinner of fresh fish and a special potato dish he had gotten two planets back. They had a wonderful dinner conversation about trans-tunnel flight and how it might be possible to take the speed of a ship up a thousand times by opening tunnels inside of tunnels.

Fisher tried to focus on the conversation and not think about how he wished Callie was sitting there with them. If he was lucky, that would happen at some point.

He wasn't sure when. But he was willing to go slow to make it happen.

CALLIE SPENT the rest of the afternoon sitting in the café, at the counter, just staring at the pictures Fisher had left with her.

She had found a magnifying glass behind the main desk in a drawer and studied them up close. They didn't seem to have been altered in any way.

And the pictures seemed to be on some sort of paper she had never felt before. Under magnification, it didn't really have a grain.

Then, as the ravine outside the window got dark, she went up and turned on lights in the main area, put Fisher's pack with the pictures behind the main counter, so she wouldn't have to look at them, then started the fire in the big fireplace.

She changed into the same sweats she had on in the picture and then made herself a light dinner. After that she just curled up on the couch, a blanket wrapped around her.

She had no idea how long she sat there thinking about her friends at the university, and about her parents who had died three years ago.

But it seemed that every other thought was about Fisher. And how he looked.

And his smile.

And how much she wanted to get to know him, just as he said he wanted to get to know her.

Slowly, she felt like the memory of the night was coming back, but she honestly wasn't sure if they were real memories or just her making something up from the pictures.

It might have been hours, but she ended up dozing.

Some whistling from the basement café area woke her up. The sun was up, but barely and the fire in the fireplace was nothing but embers.

She looked at her watch. It was 7:30 in the morning.

She scrambled for her room down the hall, took a quick shower, and put on clean jeans and one of her own blouses. The building was chilled, but she didn't care. From the looks of it, the day was going to turn warm.

She made it to the basement just at eight.

It smelled wonderful, as if someone had been cooking for hours.

The big wood table they had sat at yesterday now had napkins and silverware on it. There were two large glasses of orange juice at the table, something that the lodge did not have. He had brought the juice from somewhere.

A moment later Fisher came out of the back room carrying two plates of food.

"Good morning," he said, his smile almost melting her. Oh, my god, how could one man be so damned good-looking?

"Morning," she said, so stunned that all she could do beyond that was nod back at him.

"Grab a seat."

He sat two identical plates on the table, then he headed back to the kitchen. "Just have to get the toast."

She watched him go, then turned back to the table.

Ham, eggs, hash browns, orange juice.

She just shook her head as she took the same seat as the day before and he came back out of the kitchen smiling. "Pretty nice kitchen in there," he said as he slid the toast onto the table. "Not as good as my kitchen on *The Lady*, but pretty close."

"*The Lady*?" she asked.

"The ship my friend and I built on our home world about two years ago."

"Not one of the rescue ships?" she asked, almost afraid to touch her silverware, even though her stomach was rumbling and the food smelled wonderful.

"Oh, heavens, no," he said, laughing. "We thought our ship was big when Doc and I built it, but right now *The Lady* looks like a tiny flea in one of the big ship's landing decks. The big ship is called *The R-12* because they built it too fast to name it yet. It has about two thousand men, women, and children living on it."

Callie couldn't imagine a ship that size.

Fisher went on. "It held almost twenty thousand more, including you, in the rescue."

"Where is it from?"

"From what I have been told, a very distant section of this galaxy."

"Wow," she said, not really understanding or even imagining what he was trying to tell her in what seemed to be normal conversation.

"Yeah," Fisher said, nodding. "I honestly have no idea how really big that ship is."

"So how did you get on it?" she asked, clearly not believing she was having this conversation.

He indicated that she should eat, then he dug into his eggs before answering her.

"They saved us just as they saved you and all the survivors on this planet."

She shook her head and nibbled at a piece of wonderful toast, made from fresh bread, something she had convinced herself she would not see in any near future.

He was eating, clearly hungry. And he seemed to be in a wonderful mood.

"You said there were almost two million survivors on this planet. How could one ship save them all?"

Again he laughed softly. "There were almost one hundred of the huge ships in orbit, built just for the rescue by over fifty different human planets' cultures. *The R-12* just had over twenty thousand of the people from here."

"And not your planet?" she asked, tasting the wonderful eggs. He had a slight pepper taste on them which made them perfect.

"My planet doesn't even know Doc and I are gone. My planet is about at the same place as your planet was before this tragedy, maybe ten or twenty years behind. All the planets we visited in this area are at the same level in development, or behind where your planet was before this tragedy."

She started to ask him something and he held up his hand with his fork in it for her to stop. Then he smiled that wonderful smile. "Trust me, don't ask. Doc and I flew around out there for two years and visited almost two hundred human worlds. And I don't believe the answer to what you were about to ask. But it's part of the project I could really use your help on if you decide to take a look."

"So what is your friend doing while you are down here slumming?"

He waved an arm around the place. "Far from slumming and great company."

She smiled and kept eating, enjoying every bite. And enjoying company more than she wanted to admit, even with the strange conversations.

"Doc is working with the engineers of the big ship, more specifically a young head engineer named Kalinda. He's learning how to make our ship even faster and I have a hunch he's going to be helping them out as well."

"He's that good?"

"Better," Fisher said.

"And why aren't you there working with him?" she asked.

"Trans-tunnel drives and warp-space calculations are past me for the most part. I tend to like working to find things that are clear, but not seen in both mathematics and the real world."

"I like to do that as well, only without the mathematics," she said, smiling.

"I know," he said. "You told me that during the first night, which is another reason I think you could help me on my little quest."

"But first I have to agree to transport with you to the ship."

"Not really," he said. "You can stay right here if you want. I can bring down supplies and some very powerful computers and everything we would need to see if we can find some answers. If you wouldn't mind some company at times, that is. This place is really special and very comfortable."

"It won't be when the power goes off shortly," she said, trying to comprehend what he had said about not really needing her to go back with him if she didn't want.

He laughed. "My specialty is seeing things between other things. Between light and dark matter there is unlimited energy. The big ship uses it, I invented it for my planet, but no one took me seriously. So we built what we thought was a big spaceship and left. No one noticed."

He reached into his pocket and pulled out a small device that looked to be no bigger than an apple, with two square sides on it and terminals.

He set it on the table between them. "When the power goes off, we hook this up to the power grid for the lodge and we'll have unlimited power for as long as needed."

She stared at the small device for a moment, then said, "Why are you making this offer?"

"I'll give you full honesty," he said.

"Please."

He nodded. "Same two reasons I said yesterday. I am really attracted to you and would like a chance to get to know you better."

"Flattering," she said, and it was. Her heart was beating faster than she could remember. She was scared to death of this stranger, yet wanted to get to know him as well.

She had never been the type to go for dangerous types. And no warning signal about him was going off for her. Even though he was telling very strange and unbelievable stories, he didn't seem dangerous in the slightest.

"Second," he said, "I could really use your help on something I feel is wrong with what I have seen on that big ship and during the two years that Fisher and I flew around before coming here."

"Wrong how?" she asked, suddenly even more worried.

"Wrong with the history they are telling me and that they all believe. Since I am an outsider and you are an outsider, I think we can see things that they are not seeing, even though they are hundreds and hundreds of years more advanced than we are."

"And you wouldn't mind staying down here and working?"

"Not in the slightest," he said, smiling. "In fact, the more I'm here, the more I like this place and after seeing it yesterday, was going to suggest that even if you came back to the ship with me, we work here."

"Seriously?" she asked.

"Seriously," he said, smiling at her with that wonderful smile of his. "It will keep us from being influenced by the 'truths' they have built up in their belief systems."

"Then let's work here," she said, smiling at him. "But on a couple of conditions."

"Name them," he said, smiling as well.

"You and your people help me move the bodies that are within a half mile of this building to someplace safe and respectful to them."

He nodded, now serious. "I don't really have any people to speak of, but I think the people on the ship can do that. I would have to check."

"Good," she said. "Secondly, you show me the big ship and your ship."

At that his smile looked like it was going to break out of his face.

"When?" he asked.

"How about now, before I chicken out?"

He laughed. "I remember saying that exact same thing before I transported down here yesterday."

He reached for her arm.

His touch was gentle and sent shivers up her spine.

"Two to transport."

And the old diner around her vanished.

PART THREE

CALLIE FOUND HERSELF standing next to Fisher on a wide platform in a large room. The place was the size of two large gymnasiums and had a large number of the platforms around the outside of the space. The fact that she was standing there like that scared her more than she wanted to admit.

The big room had a clean, antiseptic smell and was colored in tans and whites, with a soft surface of some sort on the floor. It was in a very, very stark contrast to the old wooden lodge they had just been sitting in.

A short-haired woman wearing sandals and jeans came running over to the platform from a door into another room. The smile on her face seemed to be almost infectious.

"You must be Doctor Callie Sheridan," she said, extending her hand to Callie. "I'm Raina, the transport advisor who's been helping Fisher. Welcome to *The R-12.*"

"Nice to meet you as well," Callie said, shaking the woman's firm hand and then stepping down from the platform with Fisher.

Callie couldn't believe she could even talk, but her politeness gene must have kicked in overcoming the sheer terror she was feeling.

"Let me call The Chairman," Raina said, turning to a podium that had come up out of the floor facing the platform. "So he can get you special crew status and into the system."

Her fingers moved over the slick board, then Raina looked at Callie again. "Fisher can show you as much of the ship as you like, but if you ever need anything, or need to go to the planet again, just come to me."

Before Callie could say anything, Fisher asked, "Is there any way that we can get special permission to just transport to the lodge below and back, kind of like my return button under my arm, without coming in here?"

"Planning on staying there?" Raina asked, that infectious smile of hers making Callie relax just a little.

Fisher smiled. "It's beautiful in the lodge, an amazing place. A good place for us to both work."

Raina nodded. "I think we can work that out, but I'll have to get permission."

"Permission granted," a man said as he appeared out of thin air beside Raina.

Callie knew it was going to take some time for her to get used to people doing that. If Fisher hadn't gently held her elbow, she would have stumbled back right there.

The man who had just appeared looked directly at Raina. "And permission for them to take to the surface the instruments they need for their work as well."

"Understood," Raina said, smiling. "I'll work with them for whatever they need."

The new man who was clearly in charge was about Fisher's height, but a lot older, with silver hair and a wonderful smile. He extended his hand to Callie. "Welcome back to *The R-12*, Doctor Sheridan. Just call me Benson or Chairman. We were all hoping you would come and tour our little ship."

"I hear it's not so little," Callie said, smiling at Benson as she shook his hand. Her stomach was so tight, she felt she needed to just sit down. But everyone was being so nice, she did her best to stay with them, as if this were just a normal event.

"Thank you," Fisher said to Benson.

Benson laughed. "All of us on this ship are going to owe you and your partner a great amount by the time he and Kalinda are finished."

Fisher laughed. "Yeah, set Doc loose and you just never know what's going to happen.

"It's clear why you two are the first ones to explore this area of the galaxy," Benson said. "With your energy device and his grasp of trans-tunnel mechanics, no planet was ever going to hold you."

"Thank you," Fisher said, nodding and from what Callie could see, he seemed slightly embarrassed. She liked that. He didn't take compliments well.

She forced herself to take a deep breath and try to focus on what was going on.

"I have you into the system as a special crew status, Dr. Sheridan," Benson said, looking at her. "And the rest of the crew is getting a notice to answer any questions or help you in any fashion you like."

"Thank you, Mr. Chairman. And it's just Callie."

"Welcome aboard, Callie," he said. "I hope we can get a chance to talk at some point in the future."

With that he just vanished and Fisher again had to hold her elbow slightly to keep her from stepping back. She was never, ever going to get used to people just vanishing like that.

Raina was smiling as she went back to the board on the podium. "Go take the tour and I'll have your special transport buttons ready in about an hour."

"Thank you," Callie said, not knowing what to feel or say.

"I'm just glad that we could find you," Raina said, "and that you were courageous enough to come look around."

"As am I," Fisher said, smiling at Callie.

"Now, go take a tour," Raina said, turning back to her board. "I got work to do."

Fisher led them out the door and through an office with about twenty people working. Some of the closer ones looked up and said, "Welcome aboard."

And they were all smiling and actually seemed happy to have her on board. They all looked like just normal office workers, but unless Fisher was pulling a very large scam on her, this office was in orbit over her planet.

And every one of these people were aliens.

Fisher led her through to what looked like a reception area and to a wall panel. There he explained the simple commands on the panel, showing her how to find her location on the big ship.

"Now this is the fun part," Fisher said, smiling. "How about we go meet Doc and Kalinda in Engineering?"

Callie nodded, doing her best to just pay attention. She could feel she was beyond overwhelmed at this point.

"Ask for the location for engineering," Fisher said.

She turned to the board and asked and the map showed her the area.

"Now watch," he said, smiling. "I honestly don't think I can ever get tired of this."

"Two to transport to engineering."

Callie felt nothing, but an instant later they were standing in what looked like a waiting area against one wall of a huge engineering lab area.

Parts of it seemed to go off into the distance with people in white coats, mostly bent over consoles. The ceiling was high and even with dozens of people talking, the sound seemed to be dampened by something.

It looked so normal, so human to Callie, she was having a very difficult time realizing she was on a big ship from another planet.

"Doc's the tall skinny one in the middle of that group," Fisher said.

Callie took Fisher's arm. "He looks busy and I'm a little overwhelmed to be honest. How about you show me your ship after you show me the room where I was that night."

He turned to face her, suddenly worried. "I'm sorry, I know how I felt the first time I came into this ship and Doc and I had already been in space for years."

Without letting her say a word he tapped the board. "Two to transport to L-266."

Callie found herself standing next to Fisher in a large hall that looked like it could hold hundreds. Chairs and tables and cots were stacked against one inner wall.

The other wall was a floor-to-ceiling window looking out over Earth.

The scene of the planet below was stunningly beautiful with all the blues and whites and browns. Her area of the West Coast was in solid sunlight and she could almost pick out Portland and other West Coast cities.

Fisher had gone to the wall and gotten them both chairs, then he motioned that she should follow him over toward the window. At one spot he put the two chairs down facing one another.

"There were between over two hundred or so survivors in this room," he said as she sat down. "They had food against the wall on tables and medical staff back in those rooms. People were sitting and laying down everywhere. And it smelled like death."

She nodded, looking around at the room. She knew that smell too well already.

"You transported in right here in the sweats and sweatshirt," Fisher said. "When you spun around to look at the window, you fainted. The medical person said it was from not eating and shock."

"Not eating," she said, not wanting to believe that she could faint from shock. But she was feeling pretty light-headed right now, she had to admit. And she had just had a great breakfast.

Down there.

On the planet's surface.

"I happened to be nearby," Fisher said, "and I caught you and got you checked and some food."

"And we talked?" she asked, trying to remember. Everything around her had that familiar feeling, but she just couldn't put a memory to the feeling.

"We did, for about two hours," Fisher said. "Then you said you wished you could just stay here and when I went to check, the ship came back into orbit and you were transported, erasing your memory of the hours on board."

"I'm glad you came to get me," she said, reaching over and squeezing his hand. It felt wonderful and she could see in his face that he liked her touch as well.

She had no doubt that this was a very gentle man with very little experience with women. And that made him even more attractive than he already was, if that was possible.

"I'm glad you agreed to come see this place," he said.

"And now that I'm here, you still want to work in the lodge?" she asked.

"Very much," he said. "I'll explain why when we are back in the lodge."

"Fair enough," she said.

She stood and walked over closer to the big window, staring down at her planet below. The ship's orbit was taking it over parts of Europe now and she could see large areas of blackness where lights used to shine.

Earth was slowly shutting down. And there was no telling how many centuries it would take to come back to what it was, if it ever would.

She had been fantastically lucky to meet Fisher.

She turned and looked at the most handsome man she had ever seen, staring into those deep green eyes. She really, really wanted to get to know this man.

And she really, really wanted this all to be real, and that she wouldn't have to spend the winter alone in that lodge, worrying about survival every day.

"Thank you," she said.

He only nodded, clearly not sure what to say.

"Now, let's go see that ship of yours."

He smiled, a twinkle in his eyes. "With pleasure. After seeing this ship, it will be like seeing a townhouse inside a large city."

"But it's your townhouse, right?" she asked, laughing.

"Exactly," he said, grinning at her as they put the chairs back against the wall and headed for the transport panel.

She felt a lot better. Still overwhelmed, of that she had no doubt.

But after seeing the big room and imagining that night, she now was starting to believe Fisher.

And she was falling for him more and more every minute they were together.

FISHER COULDN'T BELIEVE he was showing Callie his ship. He felt like a proud parent. He tried to make the tour short, but at the same time he hoped it would last for a very long time.

Finally, after about a half hour of the control room, engine room, storage areas, and his suite, they made it back to the kitchen and dining area.

"Oh, my God," Callie said, standing in the kitchen and looking around. "This is amazing. You designed this?"

"Every detail," he said, about as proud of that statement as he had ever felt about anything he had done. "As I said, I love to cook."

"I guess so," she said, studying the details of the kitchen.

Suddenly he realized something that hadn't occurred to him before. "You are the very first person I've ever had the chance to show this ship to."

She stopped and turned to look at him, her deep brown eyes holding his gaze.

"I'm not kidding," Fisher said. "Back home we built this ship in secret in a warehouse, me and Doc doing all the work. And on all the planets we've visited, we never had guests until now. You are not the first to be in this kitchen because I cooked dinner last night for Doc and Kalinda. But you are the first to get the full tour."

"I am honored," she said, smiling at him and bowing slightly.

"Actually, the pleasure is all mine."

They stood there staring at each other for an awkward moment in the silence before Fisher finally found the nerve to speak.

"Let me fix us some lunch."

"I'd love that," Callie said. "Rest room?"

Fisher pointed down the wide corridor leading off the kitchen and along the spine of the ship. "Bathroom is the second door on the right. Look around the other rooms in there as well and tell me what you think when you get back."

She nodded and he turned to get some bread from the pantry and turkey and fixings from one of the fridges for a simple lunch. If she felt like he had felt his first time on *The R-12*, she wouldn't be able to eat much. But she needed something.

And so did he.

He sat the table and poured them both water and iced tea and had them on the table when she returned.

"That's an amazing suite," Callie said, coming into the kitchen. "Really comfortable."

"It is, isn't it?" Fisher asked, pointing to the table to indicate she should sit down.

She did as he said, "It's your suite if you want it if you need to stay up here."

"Mine?" she asked, frowning.

"I know it can't compete with that incredible old lodge, but when we are working, if you want to stay up here, that suite is yours. Doc and I have never had guests on board, even though we added seven suites similar to that one. We would love to have different company at times."

"Seven of those suites, plus your own suites? Wow, you did build this ship big."

"We thought so until we saw *The R-12*. As Benson said, space and energy are in abundant supply in space."

"And you know how to get the energy," she said, staring at him as he worked on the sandwiches.

"On my planet I invented a source of unlimited energy, yes. But no one paid any attention. They will eventually."

"What's the name of your home planet?" she asked.

Fisher took a deep breath and laughed as he finished the sandwiches and cut them into halves. "Now we're getting into the part you won't believe. And where I'm going to need some help."

"At some point you got to start telling me," she said, laughing as he set the sandwich in front of her. "I am here seeing all this. Not really believing it all, but seeing it."

He sat down, worried about what he was about to say, then just decided to go ahead and start. "It's called Earth."

She looked at him, the sandwich halfway to her mouth.

"Every planet we visited, every society, called their planet Earth, or something in their own language that meant Earth. Benson and everyone on this ship from another sector of the galaxy is also from a planet called Earth."

Her green eyes bore into him and then she just shook her head. "You aren't kidding, are you?"

"I'm not kidding, but I didn't say I was believing any of it either," he said. "But I've seen it. And if you are up for it after lunch, I can show you images of some of the many planets Doc and I visited before we came here."

"I think I might need to see some of that," she said, nodding.

And then she took a bite of her sandwich with delight, something Fisher knew he would never get tired of watching.

CALLIE LET FISHER SHOW her about an hour of recorded visits to other human planets. With each recording he showed her on a star map where the world was.

He said that she was sitting in Doc's chair and he was in his in the control room. He used the big screen between the chairs on the main panel to show her.

"We investigated mostly yellow dwarf suns like ours and yours staying in our neighborhood of the galaxy," he said. "In fact, compared to how large the galaxy is, we haven't left the home street yet in the neighborhood."

She thought she had some idea of the size of the galaxy before, but now she was starting to understand just how big it was.

After showing her about ten worlds, all about the same level of human advancement as her world and his, she had him stop. Her brain wasn't allowing anymore in.

"Background first," she said, sitting back in the comfortable command chair and closing her eyes. "How many human cultures did you visit on how many planets?"

"Just over two hundred," Fisher said.

"All were at the same level of advancement?"

"Generally, yes," Fisher said.

"How is that possible?" she asked, opening her eyes and looking at him.

"That's exactly the big question I was hoping you would help me with," Fisher said. "Something doesn't feel right about all this, but the people of the world that built *The R-12* and ran this rescue have been studying this for centuries."

"And you don't like what they have come up with as an answer?" she asked.

"Oh, the basics, I agree with," he said. "And when you are ready to hear it, there's someone on board who can help with those. She helped me. But it's as overwhelming as this."

She nodded. She was feeling completely overwhelmed.

And she wanted to know for certain that she could go back to the planet's surface when she wanted. She was trusting Fisher more and more, but now she needed that final feeling that she wasn't trapped before she could relax a little.

"How about we go meet your friend Doc, then go get our transport devices and head back to the lodge. You can give me the basics there."

"Sounds perfect," Fisher said, smiling.

On the way out, he showed her how to get into *The Lady* if she needed to, which she thought was an amazing amount of trust.

A few moments later they were standing in the engineering section of the big ship again.

This time Doc and a woman were alone, so Fisher led her toward him.

As they got close, this very skinny man glanced up and broke into a huge smile that seemed to completely fill his face and almost made his nose vanish.

The woman beside him, also tall and very skinny did the same. And they both came to greet her like she was a lost friend.

"Welcome back, Doctor Sheridan," Doc said, smiling and shaking her hand. "Very glad you decided to join this craziness."

"Callie," she said to Doc and Kalinda. "Just call me Callie."

"We heard you were on board," Doc said. "Getting the tour?"

"*The Lady* is really something," Callie said, feeling completely at ease with both of these new people. Fisher clearly had great friends and she liked them both at once.

Doc smiled like he was a kid and she had just given him a big piece of candy.

"It's going to be a lot faster pretty soon," Doc said.

"How much faster?" Fisher asked.

"Well, it would take us now about thirty hours to go the sixty light years to get home."

Fisher nodded and Callie could see that Doc and Kalinda were both bursting with pride at what Doc was about to say next.

"We can cut that to thirty minutes," Doc said, smiling.

Fisher actually seemed rocked back at that news.

"And with what we are working on," Kalinda said, "we might cut that to only seconds."

"Wow," Fisher said. "That is really something."

"We got half the room working on it now," Doc said. "I haven't had this much fun since back when we built and first tested *The Lady*."

Callie didn't know what to think. She was having a hard time just imagining so many things, let along going sixty light years in a matter of seconds.

"Well, keep going," Fisher said. "You two are really amazing."

"Thanks," Doc said. "And great meeting you, Callie. I hope we get a chance to talk at some point."

"Me too," Kalinda said.

Feeling totally stunned, Callie agreed and turned with Fisher back toward the panel on the wall. Fisher walked with her in silence, obviously stunned at what his partner was doing.

A moment later they were back in the transportation department with Raina who planted a button under Callie's skin without so much as even touching her. Callie was really impressed with that.

Then Raina did something to Fisher's control as well.

"I set both buttons for the kitchen on your ship and the front room of the lodge where you left from yesterday, Fisher."

Callie and Fisher both nodded.

Callie was having trouble even understanding that was only yesterday. She had to slow down some and catch her breath and think. Things were moving far, far too fast.

Raina went on. "Two distinct pushes take you to the lodge. One distinct push takes you to your ship's kitchen area. That way you don't have to go through here all the time."

"But we like seeing you," Fisher said, smiling.

Raina laughed. "Thanks. If you want equipment in either location for whatever you are going to work on, you will need to come to me."

"I can't thank you enough," Fisher said.

"Yes, thank you," Callie said. "It's been wonderful meeting you."

Raina gave her a hug and then whispered in her ear. "Take care of him. He's a real catch."

Callie smiled at the woman. "I hope to."

"Good," Raina said. "Now off you go. Test those buttons."

"Lodge?" Fisher asked, looking at Callie.

"Lodge," Callie said.

Then she felt for the button as Fisher vanished.

With one last smile at Raina, she pushed it twice.

And ended up standing beside Fisher in the main room of the lodge, right in front of the big front desk. The fire from last night was just embers in the fireplace and the sun was still lighting up the room.

It felt like she had been gone forever, yet it had only been a few hours.

"Well, that worked," Fisher said.

Callie moved over and dropped on the couch.

"How about I head back to the ship and give you a couple hours alone and then bring us some dinner. You up for dinner? Or do you need more time."

She looked up at the worried expression on his handsome face and smiled. "Dinner sounds wonderful."

He nodded and smiled as well. "Back in three hours."

He touched his arm and vanished.

She pulled a blanket off the back of the couch and covered herself and just lay there staring at the logs of the ceiling over her.

Numb.

None of this could be happening.

She was attracted to an alien from another planet who lived in a spaceship inside an even bigger spaceship full of really nice aliens from more planets.

And most of the people on her world were dead.

All of her old life was dead.

Yet Fisher was offering her a new life, far more exciting than her old one.

And he was so damn handsome.

She closed her eyes.

She just needed to rest and think.

Just for a short time.

34

CALLIE AWOKE AS FISHER was quietly trying to put firewood in the fireplace and get the fire started. She lay there, smiling at him as he worked to stack the wood and start it, clearly not having a clue what he was doing.

It was dark outside the windows and he was trying to start the fire while holding a flashlight in one hand.

He was amazingly good-looking and clearly in shape. He had told her he used the gym on his ship all the time, and she could tell that he did just from how he moved with the grace of someone in shape and control of his body.

And he was also clearly a very considerate and sweet man. That had been obvious from the first moment she had met him. Raina was right, he was a catch.

"Not the outdoors type?" she asked, not moving from her position on her side on the couch.

He glanced back. "I'm sorry," he said. "I didn't mean to wake you. Just wanted to get a fire started and let you sleep. After everything today, you need it."

She sat up and stretched, realizing as she pushed the blanket back just how chilly the lodge had become. No wonder he was working on the fire for her.

"I did need that," she said, stretching and yawning again. "But you promised me dinner, remember?"

He laughed. "I did. It's downstairs."

"If I get the fire started, can we eat it up here?"

"Easily," he said.

"Light switch near the staircase for the overhead lights," she said as she stood. "I'm going to splash some water on my face and then I'll get the fire going."

"I'll be back up in ten minutes with dinner," he said, smiling at her in the light of his flashlight.

On the way down he flipped on the overhead lights.

"Power's still on?" she asked as she headed for the hallway.

"Nope," he said as he vanished down the stairs.

She just shook her head. The entire lodge was being powered by a cube the size of a saltshaker that he had invented on another planet. How was this perfect man even real?

She had the fire going strong and lights around the lodge turned on when Fisher brought the dinner up the stairs on two plates balanced on a large tray with two glasses of some juice and a bottle of water.

It smelled heavenly, like a wonderful pot roast that had simmered all day in the oven.

She went over and sat down in one of the big overstuffed chairs, pulling it closer to the big wooden coffee table where he set dinner.

He sat in another chair facing her and said, "Hope you like a very tender steak."

She could tell the steak had been sliced thin with a sampling of white sauce along one edge. Fresh asparagus spears were coated in a light cheese sauce and some tiny red potatoes coated in butter filled the rest of the plate.

"Oh, my, this is wonderful," she said. "And it smells heavenly."

"Dig in," he said, grabbing his fork and knife and easily cutting the steak on his plate.

While they ate, they talked about her past and his past, both mentioning their parents. She learned how long he and Doc had been friends and how they had been laughed at for their projects.

She understood that feeling and had seen it a number of times where she taught. Professors could sometimes be so petty that it had stunned her.

She liked the fact that he was willing to tell her about his home and his money and how he and Doc had built *The Lady*.

"What did you expect to find when you left?" she asked.

"Honestly, not much," he said, finishing up the last bite of potato on his plate. "We hoped to find some alien life, maybe plants, on different planets, that sort of thing. We were just out exploring with every intention of going home when we got bored."

"That didn't happen," she said, laughing.

"Actually, it almost did," Fisher said, sitting back in the big chair. "After a couple hundred Earth-like planets with all human civilizations about the same level, it was getting boring."

Now that surprised her. And the idea that all those planets were at the same level bothered her more than she wanted to admit.

"I'm still not seeing how that is possible," she said, shaking her head as she finished the last bit of her steak and pushed the plate away. "And that was a wonderful dinner. Thank you."

He smiled. "You are more than welcome. Not often I get a chance to really cook for someone besides Doc, who tends to eat everything."

"And he stays that skinny?" Callie asked, again feeling stunned.

"Drives me crazy because he doesn't exercise," Fisher said, shaking his head. "I'm in the gym three hours a day on most days because I love it and I like to eat like this. Doc never exercises and yet eats all of my cooking and doesn't gain a pound."

Callie laughed. She was falling for this man even more with every passing minute.

Fisher stood and started gathering up the dishes. "Let me take care of these dishes, get them washing, and we can talk if you like, or call it a night. Up to you."

She didn't want him to leave yet, since her brain seemed to be slowly returning. "Let's talk for a time."

"Would you like some tea or wine?"

"You have wine?" she asked, surprised.

"Red or white, some great choices from about twenty different planets," he said, his smile filling his face.

"A glass of red would be wonderful," she said. "Not too heavy."

"Got a perfect one," he said.

He put her dishes on the tray, leaving behind her half-finished tea and the bottle of water. "Be right back."

Balancing the tray with one arm, he pinched his arm and vanished.

She just sat there staring at the space where he had been standing a moment before. "Callie, what have you gotten yourself into?"

Only the crackling of the fire answered her back.

She stood and headed for her suite to change into a pair of slippers, turning on the music to a low level to cut the silence.

She sort of had a date for a drink with a man from space.

And she was looking forward to it.

35

FISHER FOUND DOC and Kalinda sitting in the kitchen of *The Lady* when he jumped back to get the wine. They were both eating sandwiches and had data pads on the table between them. Clearly it was a working dinner for them, which didn't surprise Fisher at all. Doc seldom didn't work.

"Dinner with Callie, huh?" Doc asked.

Fisher nodded, putting the dishes to one side of the sink.

"How's she doing with all this?" Kalinda asked.

"Actually adjusting pretty well. I haven't really tried to explain the Seeders to her yet, though. Not sure if I completely understand them myself."

"Yeah, good luck with that," Kalinda said, shaking her head. "I grew up with this knowledge, I can only faintly imagine what it must feel like to just be learning all this."

"It's weird," Doc said, smiling at Kalinda.

"Very," Fisher said. "I'm going to head back down. If you need me, Raina in transportation knows exactly where I am."

"Have fun," Doc said.

Kalinda just smiled as Fisher turned and headed back into the pantry to get the wine and a couple of glasses.

A moment later he was standing back in the big main room of the lodge.

The fire was going strong, there was faint music in the background, and Callie was seated in one chair facing the fire.

"Thanks for the great dinner," she said as he opened the wine and poured it, then took another one of the overstuffed chairs facing the fire and half turned to face her as well.

"My complete pleasure," he said.

They spent the next thirty minutes just talking more about their families and how her parents had been killed in a plane accident. Then she finally turned the big chair to face him more.

"Okay, you've been avoiding telling me about what you want me to help you with. Time to get to that."

He nodded and sat his glass of wine down on the coffee table.

"Now please realize that I've only been seeing this for myself for a few years now, and only had a nice person named Jenny on the ship try to explain it to me just yesterday."

"So we both have fresh eyes on this." Callie said.

"Exactly," Fisher said. Then he took a deep breath and started into this explanation that might lose him Callie. But at this point, he had no choice at all.

He explained how he felt while he and Doc were seeing all the civilizations at the same level. Then he told her Jenny's explanation of how a race they called "The Seeders" seeded all the human planets in the galaxy and then left.

"Aren't there something like one hundred billion stars in this galaxy?" Callie asked, shaking her head.

"Closer to two hundred billion," Fisher said. "A large part of those are outside of what our astronomers called 'the habitable zone' for human life, meaning they are too close in toward the center of the galaxy. And the vast majority of stars in this galaxy are red dwarfs, not yellow dwarfs as our sun. And a few of the yellow dwarfs Doc and I found didn't have planets in what our astronomers called 'The Goldilocks Zone' meaning inside an area where it wasn't too hot or too cold for life."

Callie just nodded. "That still would leave a lot of stars and human planets."

Fisher nodded. "More than I want to think about. Hundreds and hundreds of millions at least."

Then he went on to tell her what Jenny had told him about how the Seeders had wiped all older life from the planet with a big asteroid impact, then basically planted all animal and human life over a period of a few thousand years in numbers of visits to each planet.

Callie just shook her head. "Too much."

Fisher just nodded. "Do I understand that feeling. How about tomorrow you and I go talk with Jenny and then I can tell you what is really bothering me."

"Besides the fact that this changes every belief I've ever had and it is impossible to boot."

"Yeah, besides that," Fisher said, smiling.

CALLIE SAT, sipping the wonderful glass of red wine and letting herself relax. They had changed the conversation away from all the strange stuff and had it back on more normal stuff.

Fisher had asked her about her two days in the cave and exactly what she had been looking for and then seemed actually interested as she explained. His green eyes kept looking at her.

She was so attracted to him, it almost felt unnatural. She had never really felt like this for any other person before and she wasn't sure if it was because of the situation or simply because he seemed to be the perfect person for her.

After talking about her cave dig, they talked about exercising and he told her about his former weight problem. The fact that he had dropped it all and kept it all off impressed her even more.

She desperately wanted to ask if he had had girlfriends in the past, but didn't.

And he didn't ask her about any of her short relationships either, which she was thankful for.

Finally, after almost two hours of talking and after the entire bottle of wine was gone, he said, "I suppose I had better get back and let you get some sleep."

"Stay," she said.

She was surprised that word had come out of her mouth, and he looked surprised as well.

"There is a suite across from my suite down the hall here," she said. "You offered me a suite in your ship, it's the least I can offer in return."

He smiled.

She went on before he could politely decline. "Besides, to be honest, it would feel good to have someone else in the building."

"Now that I understand," he said, smiling. "I would love to stay. And breakfast on *The Lady* in the morning?"

"Wonderful," she said, feeling excited at the idea that he would be close by.

She led him down the hall and into the suite across from hers. The bed there was freshly made up, ready for guests that would now never come.

It had a small sitting room to one side and a large bathroom with tile floors like hers. Plus a huge bed in the bedroom with wooden posts carved out of pine trees.

He went over to the bed and pushed on it, then smiled at her and sat on it. "A real featherbed?"

"Seems they are in every room in the place," she said, smiling.

She really, really wanted to go over and sit on the bed beside him and kiss him, but she didn't.

"So you'll be all right here?" she asked.

"It's wonderful," he said, smiling at her. "Thanks."

She then said goodnight and as she started to pull the door closed he said, "It's all right to leave it open."

So she did, going back to her suite.

She once again got into the sweat pants and sweatshirt she now wore to bed, then crawled in and shut off the light. She could hear him moving around a little, then silence.

She lay there, staring up into the darkness. Out the window, she could see some stars up through the pine trees. They seemed bright and welcoming now, for some reason.

What in the world was she doing? The man of her dreams was across the hallway. He had flat told her he was attracted to her. And he was so damned shy and respectful of her feelings, any move for them to be together would be up to her.

"Callie," she said softly to the darkness, "this is stupid."

She pushed back the heavy quilt and sheet, found her slippers, and headed out into the hallway.

His door was open but the light was off. The only light was one they had left on in the big room, plus the last light flickering from the fireplace.

She had only known this man, this alien, for a few days. Yet this felt right. That might be the half bottle of wine talking, but she didn't care.

She eased open his door and whispered, "Fisher?"

"Yes," he said from the bed.

Before she lost her nerve, she walked to the bed and slid in beside him.

"Just hold me if you wouldn't mind."

"I will never mind," he said softly.

She turned her back to him and he wrapped his arms around her and she snuggled back against him. Except for a pair of underwear, he was naked.

"This is wonderful," she said as his strong arms held her. "Thank you."

He kissed her softly on the neck. "Thank you. Now rest."

She tried.

She really tried.

But those firm arms, that fantastic body pressed against her just were impossible to resist.

Finally, she rolled over and kissed him.

And he kissed back.

She got lost in his kiss. Like no other she had ever felt. Gentle, yet insistent.

She could feel his arousal as he kissed her and she stroked his naked shoulders.

Under the big quilt and sheet it was getting warm. Too damn warm, actually, to be wearing as many clothes as she was wearing.

Finally she pulled away from one more fantastic and long kiss, panting.

Then she pushed the covers back, stood, and turned on the lamp next to the bed. She took off the sweatshirt and sweatpants as Fisher watched, his eyes wide and his smile big.

"You are fantastically beautiful," he said, his voice slightly raspy.

"Get rid of those pants," she said.

And he did.

Then she crawled back in bed with him, kissing him and letting him feel her body against his and guiding his hands to places they needed to go.

She hadn't been with very many men before, but it had never, ever come close to how wonderful making love to Fisher was.

She belonged with him. She knew it and she felt it.

Almost two hours later they finally dozed off in each other's arms, only the sheet pulled up over them.

And even with everything that had happened, she felt safer than she had ever felt in her life.

37

CALLIE AWOKE as Fisher was working to ease himself away from her. The morning light was just starting to brighten up the trees outside the window and she felt wonderful, better than she could ever remember feeling waking up. She normally wasn't a morning person.

As Fisher moved, she turned and pulled him in close and kissed him, long and hard.

And he kissed her in return, just as hard and just as passionately.

The man could kiss. The two of them just fit perfectly together. How was that even possible?

"Where did you think you were going, mister?" she asked after letting him come up for air from the kiss.

"Get us some food," he said, smiling at her.

"Not yet," she said, kissing him.

She could feel his body had the same idea as hers.

She climbed on top of him and they made love again, quick and intense and even more incredible than the night before.

Finally, as they both lay there trying to catch their breaths, she raised up on her elbow and looked into his wonderful green eyes. "I hope I wasn't too forward."

He laughed. "One of us needed to be and I was too damn scared to even suggest anything."

"And why am I so scary?" she asked, smiling.

"Because you are the most beautiful woman I have ever met," he said, looking directly into her eyes with those intense green eyes of his. "And the smartest and bravest."

"You know the exact right thing to say to a woman."

"Just the truth," he said. "Just the truth."

She kissed him long and hard once again, then rolled out of bed and picked up her sweat pants and sweatshirt, standing there naked in front of him. "I'm going to take a long, hot shower and get dressed. I'll meet you on *The Lady* for that promised breakfast?"

"Perfect," he said.

With one last look at the naked man stretched out on the bed staring at her, she turned and headed out the door and across the hallway.

Thirty minutes later, she pushed her transport button under her skin and appeared in *The Lady's* kitchen.

Fisher was already there dressed in fresh clothes and with wet hair, working on starting to cook something.

"You are right," she said. "I don't think this transport thing will ever get old."

He laughed, put down what he was working on and came over and kissed her long and hard. Then he finally pulled away and said, "Sit and I'll cook."

"I feel like I should do something to help," she said, moving over to the table and sitting.

"Eggs, ham, hash browns, toast, and juice," he said, smiling at her and making her want to just jump back up and kiss him again. "Not much to help with. But I could use your feedback on a few things."

"That was really nice last night," she said, staring at his broad shoulders and tight butt in the jeans.

"Nice doesn't begin to describe it for me," he said, smiling. "Thank you for taking the chance."

She laughed. "I doubt I would have gotten much sleep there in my own bed alone with you so close."

"I was feeling the same way when you came in," he said, smiling over his shoulder at her as he worked on starting the hash browns in a small pan.

"So what can I give you feedback on?" she asked.

At that moment, before he had a chance to answer, Doc and Kalinda came in. Both of them looked like they had just gotten out of the shower and Kalinda was wearing the same clothes she had on yesterday.

"Good morning," Fisher said to the new arrivals, indicating that they should sit at the table with Callie.

She smiled at both of them and then winked at Kalinda, who just smiled fondly back at her. Callie knew that feeling. She was feeling it right now herself.

"Sure I can't help now?" Callie asked.

"Nope, just twice as much of a very simple breakfast is all. Thanks."

"So are you starting to believe all this craziness?" Doc asked Callie as he and Kalinda sat at the table holding hands.

"Still in shock about a lot of it," she said. "But another day or so and it will all just feel strange instead of completely impossible."

"How did it go yesterday with the new drive equations?" Fisher asked.

Callie could see both Doc and Kalinda brighten up, as if their minds were returning to their bodies.

"We should have the speed of *The Lady* up so that we could be back in our home system in thirty seconds," Doc said.

Callie watched as Kalinda nodded.

Fisher just shook his head in clear amazement.

"And *The R-12*," Kalinda said, "should be able to cover the six hundred light year journey home in a few days once everything is upgraded and tested."

"How long did it take you to get here?" Callie asked.

"Fourteen months," Kalinda said. "And we barely made it in time."

Callie watched as suddenly Fisher turned around, staring at Kalinda.

Callie stood and went over to him and took the spatula out of his hands and worked the eggs. She could tell he had suddenly gone into his own mind, thinking, and if she didn't take over, the breakfast was going to burn.

He started to object, but instead she pushed him toward the table. "Sit, I got this."

He nodded. Then as he sat down, he said, "Maybe using all four of you as a sounding board would be a good idea."

"Fire away," Doc said. "I'm not going anywhere until that wonderful-smelling breakfast is served."

"Glad to help," Kalinda said.

Callie nodded to Fisher that he should go on as she put the toast down and turned over the hash browns.

He started to say something, then just shook his head. "Never mind, the answer I'm looking for is obvious."

He stood and came to help Callie finish with breakfast. Then when all four of them were sitting at the table and eating, Callie had to keep the conversation going.

"So what's so obvious?"

Fisher looked at her and shrugged. "Everyone wonders how the Seeders could have done what they did and just left, moving on to another galaxy."

"Is that the theory?" Callie asked and Fisher and Kalinda both nodded.

"They left cultures to fend for themselves?" she asked, clearly not understanding what he was saying.

"That's what everyone believes on this ship, right?" Fisher asked Kalinda.

"That's what we were taught in school," she said, working on her ham.

"Not possible," Callie said and Fisher smiled at her. "None of these human cultures could have come up in such exact ways and so close in development and technology without a vast amount of guidance. Especially through the really tough turning points."

"Exactly," Fisher said, smiling. "What's obvious is that the Seeders, at least some of them, never left."

Kalinda just shook her head, now the one having trouble believing the facts in front of her. Callie felt good that it just wasn't her for a change.

"Then where are they?" Kalinda asked.

"Right here," Fisher said, waving at the entire table. "We're Seeders. Or we will be when we get a little more advanced."

Kalinda shook her head. "That theory has been considered and discarded a number of times over the years."

"No hard evidence, right?" Fisher asked.

She nodded.

Callie knew, without a doubt that the hard evidence was the simple fact that so many cultures had grown at the same pace, in exactly the same way.

Fisher looked at Kalinda who had stopped eating. "Think about it. Your culture has pretty much invented everything needed to be a seeder. And you built ships that held over two million humans on short notice."

Again Kalinda nodded, a little more slowly.

Doc was keeping out of the conversation, which Callie thought to be very smart.

"From what I have read of the articles that Jenny gave me," Fisher said, "looking for Seeders seems to have always been an outwardly directed hunt. But Callie and I have specialties that allow us to be able to see things where there isn't supposed to be anything."

Callie was honored that Fisher included her. What she was seeing didn't seem to be hidden.

"So what evidence have we all missed for a thousand years of studying this?" Kalinda asked.

Callie was glad that Fisher just ignored the barbed question and went on calmly while eating. "Assume the Seeders are humans just like us. Any evidence would be human evidence."

"We've thought of that," she said. "I can give you some of the papers discounting those theories. We got them all in basic school."

"Written by Seeders, of course," Fisher said, smiling at her frown.

Then not giving her a chance to go on, he said, "Just look at the cultures. Now I know math, and I wouldn't want to even try to calculate the chance that every culture on every Earth-like planet would become over centuries of war and fighting a democracy and a capitalism-based culture. Or that every planet would develop along the same exact lines and at the same basic speed."

Fisher turned to Callie. "Doctor, in your expertise, could cultures of any animal species, separated by light years of distance, develop at exactly the same pace and way and genetic mutation?"

"Not a chance," Callie said, smiling at Fisher. "Not without a lot of help. Vast amounts of help, actually."

"So every culture we visited was directed and helped?" Doc asked. "That's your theory?"

Fisher laughed. "It's the only thing that explains anything I've seen in the last two years. And what I see on this big ship as well. The Seeders are still here and still helping and you've met them."

Now it was Callie's turn to be shocked.

Both Doc and Kalinda were flat staring at Fisher.

"And just how are you so certain of that?" Kalinda asked, clearly upset. Callie could tell that Fisher was challenging one of her hardest held beliefs.

"Because I've met one as well," Fisher said.

Fisher glanced up at the ceiling and said just slightly louder, "Am I correct, Mr. Chairman?"

At that moment Benson shimmered into view. He pulled over a chair and sat down at the head of the table.

"Smells wonderful," he said.

"You hungry?" Fisher asked, clearly not surprised at all that Benson was sitting there with them.

Callie was shocked, but she managed to somehow just take a deep breath and watch Fisher.

"Nope, already had breakfast," Benson said. "So what gave me away?" He was smiling and ignoring the completely shocked look on Kalinda's face. Callie watched as Kalinda's mouth was opening and closing and nothing was coming out. Callie knew that feeling well from the last few days.

"A couple of slips," Fisher said. "You knew about me and Doc ahead of time."

Benson laughed. "I had hoped you had missed that. Not sure what I was thinking on that."

"And the look in your eyes when you looked at the planet below. It was a personal failure to you that you couldn't save everyone."

Benson nodded. Callie could see that Benson's eyes filled with sadness. Fisher was right. Benson did take all that death down on her world personally.

"It was my failure. This area of the region is mine to watch and I just couldn't mount a rescue operation fast enough, get the right people on advanced enough planets involved quick enough, get them here fast enough. At least we saved some of those poor souls."

"The speed of the travel to where *The R-12's* home world was another thing that gave you away. How long ahead did you know what was going to happen?" Fisher asked, his voice respectful.

Callie was impressed.

"A good three hundred years," Benson said, his voice soft. "We had to push culture advance on a number of planets faster than we wanted to even save as many as we did.

Then he looked directly at Fisher and shook his head. "I knew from the moment you two started building your ship that you would be problems."

Fisher laughed and Doc looked stunned.

"I think your secret is safe with the four of us," Fisher said.

Everyone at the table nodded.

"But I'm betting the really big problem for you is Doc and Kalinda here, right?" Fisher asked, smiling at his best friend who was really looking puzzled.

Benson nodded. He turned to Doc and Kalinda. "You two are a rare combination and very advanced. This galaxy isn't supposed to develop the kind of speed you two are working on for another two thousand years. It's about then we'll be needing help in the major part of Andromeda."

And Benson turned to Callie and Fisher. "And you two worry me even more. We could really use you both, to be honest."

"So you can use a little help a little earlier?" Fisher asked.

Callie was just flat stunned. Now she completely understood what Fisher was talking about. Benson was a member of the race of humans who started humans on all the different planets, including hers.

And now Fisher was saying that the main force of the Seeders had moved on to a completely different galaxy.

Benson laughed. "Seems like we're going to get it even if we don't need it, huh? But before then, we could use help here in the Milky Way if you four are up for the task. There are a lot of wars going on right now on the developing planets. And there's only so many of us to go around who stayed behind to help here."

"To make sure all the cultures develop to a peaceful way of life," Callie asked, trying to imagine the vastness of that task.

Benson nodded.

"So if the four of us agree to help," Fisher asked, "how long until you teach us that teleportation trick and the long-age secret?"

Callie was now completely lost again.

Benson just shook his head. "You don't miss anything, do you?"

Then he addressed the entire table. "You all agree to become a Seeder and it might be a lot sooner than later."

With that he smiled at Kalinda's open mouth and stood.

He turned to Fisher and extended his hand. "I'll let you explain what just happened," he said. "But do it down in the lodge where no one can overhear you. I've got a war to try to stop about fifty light years from here. We can all talk tomorrow if you want."

With that he vanished.

And the silence in the kitchen of *The Lady* was so thick, Callie figured she could cut it with a knife.

38

FISHER LOOKED AROUND at the three people sitting over a mostly finished breakfast in the kitchen of *The Lady*. His three friends were shocked, to say the least.

Doc looked at him. "You want to explain to me what just happened?"

Fisher nodded. "I will, just not here."

"Four to transport," Fisher said, and pushed his button under his skin for the lodge.

All four of them ended up in front of the big desk in the main room. There was a bite to the air, since the sun hadn't really hit the valley floor yet to warm up the place.

"I'll get the fire going a little," Callie said as Fisher indicated that Kalinda and Doc take a seat on the couches.

"This place is really amazing," Kalinda said, looking around. "Really, really comfortable-feeling. I love the feel of the big logs."

"That it is," Callie said.

Fisher went over and sat in one of the big chairs, saying nothing until Callie had the fire coming back up and she had sat near him on a couch.

"What just happened," Fisher said, "is that a Seeder asked us to become Seeders and help them with directing all the civilizations in this galaxy in their growth. And then maybe eventually go on and help them in Andromeda and beyond."

Kalinda just shook her head. "As a child I learned that the Seeders were mythical advanced people who built entire civilizations and then left."

"They are," Fisher said.

"As with any garden that is planted," Callie said, "it must be tended to grow the way the gardener wanted."

"And they want us to join them, help them tend the garden of all these civilizations they have planted," Kalinda said.

"That's it in a nutshell," Fisher said, nodding.

"And what do we get out of doing that?" Doc asked.

Fisher smiled at his friend. "Well, for starters, I'm betting that Benson is a few thousand years old at least."

"You're kidding me?" Doc said.

"We can ask him tomorrow," Fisher said, smiling at his friend and then looking at Callie who clearly just realized that as well. "And he basically said that if we join the Seeders and help out, we'll live a very long time as well."

Now Doc only shook his head.

"Second," Fisher said, "I'm guessing that he has the ability to transport over great distances without mechanical help. He seemed to hint as much."

"Now that would be cool as well," Doc said, nodding.

"So we can't say anything about this. Remember? We can talk with Benson tomorrow."

Doc shrugged and smiled at Kalinda. "You up for going and working on some engines?"

She smiled back and took his hand as they both stood. "I would love that, but first I want a tour of this wonderful lodge."

Callie gladly gave them a tour and Fisher jumped back to *The Lady* to do the dishes. Twenty minutes later, Callie brought Doc and Kalinda back up from the surface and then after they left, she sat at the table and watched him finish up.

When he was done, he turned to her.

"What would you like to do today?" she asked, smiling at him.

He could tell that even though it was still early in the morning, she was already overwhelmed. He was as well, to be honest.

"How about we go back to the lodge and just curl up on a couch and do nothing until lunch?"

"Perfect," she said. "Then what?"

"We come back up here, have lunch, and return to the couch."

"Perfect," she said, smiling. "And then what?".

"We come up here and have dinner and then return to the couch in front of the fire with a bottle of wine and a promise of a featherbed."

She smiled at him. "Have I ever told you how I like how you think?"

He moved over, helped her stand, kissing her long and hard, and then transported them to the lodge and the big couch in front of the fire.

39

OVER THE NEXT MONTH, as *The Lady* was having her engines upgraded and her shields worked on, Doc and Kalinda moved into the
lodge with Fisher and Callie. Doc was going to end up being right. *The
Lady* would be the fastest thing flying in any part of the galaxy.

All four of them had met with Benson on the second day and
he had made his offer clear. He wanted all four of them to become
Seeders and work together to help civilizations walk a moderately
peaceful path toward the future. They had all agreed.

Callie loved the company and with Fisher doing a lot of the cooking in the lodge kitchen and them meeting all the time in the dining
area, the lodge felt like it was actually alive.

A crew from *The R-12* had cleared out all the bodies around or
near the lodge, moving them to a respectful place down in the valley
below. So as the fall days got shorter, Callie and Fisher had started
taking walks along the road and on some of the trails.

Callie loved those walks through the crisp mountain air.

She actually had come to love this lodge a great deal, even though it was the most isolated place on a very injured planet. But with her ability to jump up into space to *The R-12*, and the other three around, she didn't feel the isolation.

One evening, as *The Lady's* engine and shield upgrades were nearing completion, Fisher seemed bothered and worried about something. Callie decided she would just wait and let him tell her.

They were walking along the roadway, both wearing coats against the crisp of the fall air. She could almost see her breath in the clear air.

"I've just assumed," Fisher said, clearly working up the courage to ask the next question, "that you would want to come along on this crazy new world and be with me. But I never really asked. Are you sure you want to join me out there?"

Callie stopped and somehow managed not to laugh. She turned Fisher so she could look him directly in the eyes.

"I love you," she said.

"I love you as well," he said. "You know that."

"You have saved me," she said, "and given me a new life where I can help millions and millions of people to find a new life as well."

He nodded.

"Of course I want to go with you. But on one condition."

"Name it," he said, looking worried.

"For as long as we are still in this galaxy, we keep this lodge up and come back here once in a while."

He broke into a huge smile.

Wow, did she love that smile and that man and the brain behind those intense green eyes.

"I have another idea as well," he said, smiling at her.

"I'm listening."

"Assuming you don't get tired of me after a few years of traveling around in space all over this galaxy helping people..."

"Yeah, that's going to happen," she said, laughing.

"Then maybe, in a couple of years, we can talk with Benson and come back here and have him marry us."

Callie just stared at the man of her dreams, her mouth open. She wasn't really sure she had heard that right.

"Well?" he asked, smiling.

"Vardis Fisher, are you asking me to marry you?"

He smiled. "I am. Too forward? Too soon?"

She grabbed him around the neck and kissed him as hard as she had ever kissed anyone before.

Then she leaned back, not letting him go. "How about having Benson marry us before we set off to save the galaxy?"

His smile now was radiating.

"I'd like that," he said.

She would like that more than she had ever imagined.

And with that they stood there in the road to the old mountain lodge, kissing, until the chill of the evening air finally drove them inside and to the big featherbed.

ABOUT THE AUTHOR

USA TODAY BESTSELLING AUTHOR Dean Wesley Smith has published more than a hundred novels in thirty years and hundreds and hundreds of short stories across many genres.

He wrote a couple dozen *Star Trek* novels, the only two original *Men in Black* novels, Spider-Man and X-Men novels, plus novels set in gaming and television worlds. He wrote novels under dozens of pen names in the worlds of comic books and movies, including novelizations of a dozen films, from *The Final Fantasy* to *Steel* to *Rundown*.

He now writes his own original fiction under just the one name, Dean Wesley Smith. In addition to his upcoming novel releases, his monthly magazine called *Smith's Monthly* premiered October 1, 2013, filled entirely with his original novels and stories.

Dean also worked as an editor and publisher, first at Pulphouse Publishing, then for VB Tech Journal, then for Pocket Books. He now plays a role as an executive editor for the original anthology series *Fiction River.*

For more information about his work, go to www.deanwesleysmith. com, www.smithsmonthly.com or www.fictionriver.com.

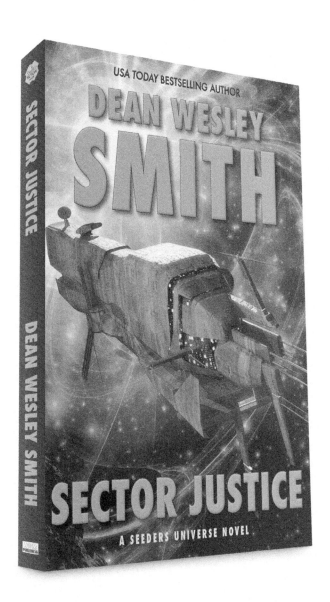

THE ADVENTURES CONTINUE IN THE NEXT
BOOK IN THE SEEDERS UNIVERSE SERIES,
SECTOR JUSTICE, AVAILABLE NOW

Made in the USA
Las Vegas, NV
16 March 2022

45753539R00121